ODOACER
A Novel

Vincent Sinjenour

Copyright © 2019 Vincent Sinjenour

All rights reserved.

ISBN: 9781709223655

To LC & AMG

A Note on the Title

Flavius Odoacer was the last barbarian general to depose a Western Roman emperor. Afterwards, he rejected the political traditions of that rickety state by declining to assume for himself either the imperial title or whatever nominal responsibilities still came with it. Because of that decision, the year of his triumph – 476 – marks the end of the Western Empire in our history books.

Odoacer accomplished all of this with the connivance and material support of the Eastern Roman Empire, which was glad to be rid of a rival power.

ACKNOWLEDGMENTS

I thank JC, LS and AE for their encouragement, CS, EB, JD and EL for their assistance, RG for financial support while I was writing this, my wife for her patience, and my daughter for her toleration.

PROLOGUE

On April 3, beginning at precisely 7:53 a.m., eastern, three tweets by the President of the United States cast a cloud of doubt over the nation's relationship with the Republic of South Africa, which had theretofore been good. The occasion was the temporary exhibition of a gemstone, known as the Cape Town Sapphire, at the American Museum of Natural History in New York.

The first tweet focused the reader's attention on the humiliation of having the American heirloom "leant" to the United States five years after its repatriation. Prior to that, the sapphire had rested 100 years in a mid-tier American museum located in the Midwest. It had been returned as a good will gesture, from one democratic republic to another, in acknowledgement of — and as amends for — certain American citizens' roles in its a murky and disreputable provenance, which involved forced labor, land seizures, and, it was said, murder.

The tweet read:

The Capetown Diamond has been in an American museum since 1918. It was donated by a great philanthropist.

ODOACER

> Millions have seen and enjoyed it. Now it's "on loan" from South Africa! DISGRACE!

This tweet raised the spirits of Andrew Radnor, 30, of Ellsworth, Maine. Earlier that month his girlfriend had left him, and the day before he'd seen her in town with another guy. At a local bar one night prior to the tweet, he'd confided to a stranger, in words or effect: "We were together for two years. It was, like, a perfect match. Everyone said we were great together. And now she'd slutting around town with this Chinese guy. It's fucking—humiliating."

"I know, Pres," said Andrew, pulling on a red cap and trundling down the porch. "I know."

The second Presidential tweet addressed the prior administration, which had arranged the repatriation of the sapphire. This was framed as a colossal betrayal of American interests and traditions. The tweet read:

> Generations of Missourians—a state I won—grew up knowing they could see the Diamond in their great Science Museum. Now it's gone because prior admin wanted to "apologize" for American Greatness. #Stabbed in the Back

Bill Fisher, 41, of Canton, Ohio, chuckled when he read this. He'd been saying almost exactly the same thing, not a day earlier. In his case, it had been a beloved Dairy Queen franchise that had been forced to close due to a combination of environmental violations and non-payment of taxes. What Bill had in fact said — to his brother-in-law, while watching a game — was: "It was always there, you know. I could always. Well, I guess the government's got to fuck that up too. Sometimes it feels. These guys aren't even on our side."

Bill stood before the door-length mirror in his mother's bedroom and adjusted his red hat. "Goddamn shame," he said.

2

ODOACER

The third Presidential tweet was by far the most provocative. It was less grievance, more threat:

> As COMMANDER IN CHIEF, I have full, Constitutional power to defend America's interest, including its SACRED HONOR. I am examining all options with my Generals and National Security Advisor Cooley. #Bring It Back

Mike Cresco, 23, of Nashville felt a flutter in his heart. Just moments ago, his breakfast had been interrupted by loud salsa music emanating from the home of his new neighbors. He'd first told his wife, "goddamn it, if they don't cut that out, I'm going to get my gun," but she'd urged caution in any number of ways, prompting him to agree: "Fine, I'll call the cops first. But if this doesn't stop soon." Whereupon he'd patted the lump in his pocket that was putatively his gun.

"See?" cried Mike, leaning over the red hat that lay on the breakfast table in order to speak almost directly into his wife's ear. "That's how we do things." His wife nodded and gently brushed him aside.

The tweets had prompted consternation and outrage on the morning shows. Reporters called their administration contacts to request clarification. Former staffers vied with the President's opponents on live TV to interpret what he had really meant by the last tweet — whether it was a threat to seize the gem, whether national honor was a constitutionally-sanctioned justification for certain executive actions, whether it was in any event advisable. A deputy press secretary gave a statement at 10 suggesting the whole thing was a joke. The Director of Homeland Security effectively contradicted that at 10:30, suggesting that the administration was in negotiations of some sort with South Africa. But another press flack came on an hour later to say she'd just spoken to the President, that he was serious, and that he'd be making an official pronouncement of his thinking on the matter on this or that appointed day.

3

ODOACER

By the next day, April 4, the staff, the bureaucracy, and the loudest of the loyalists from the President's party in Congress had all more or less settled on the narrative that the President had strengthened his bargaining position, that he was in fact bargaining for something important if undisclosed, and that serious ethical questions — raised the previous afternoon on a conspiracy website — hovered over the earlier administration's contacts with South Africa.

This prompted a round of analysis and speculation on the news networks, which had now had time to select suitable legal scholars to either confirm or demolish the legality of whatever it was the President was threatening to do, and international experts to discuss the foreign policy implications. A Congressman from the opposition party became especially incensed on one show, alleging — in the face of what the press was now treating as overwhelming vagueness — that the President of the United States had asserted constitutional authority to employ the national security apparatus to steal a sapphire from a foreign nation. This, the Congressman, a former federal prosecutor, asserted, was wrong. If the President did that, he said, Congress would impeach him.

The outburst was unseemly. Anchors and commentators across the spectrum roundly condemned the Congressman for putting words in the President's mouth. The President's supporters complained he was undermining the negotiations, which might as well have been scheduled for real, and that the Congressman wanted America to fail and be humiliated. The Congressional leaders from the Congressman's own party, nervously courting undecided moderate voters in an upcoming election, expressed regret over the Congressman's rush to judgment on the issue of impeachment — but not so much regret, they hoped, that they would alienate the activists.

Against that backdrop, the Chief of Staff called a press gaggle on the afternoon of April 5. He smiled indulgently, called the Congressman's talk "irresponsible," and assured everyone that serious discussions with South Africa were currently underway. Asked by a particularly irritating reporter whether the President, in fact, was willing to use "non-diplomatic means" to secure the "return" of the Cape Town Sapphire — the necessity of which was now taken for granted — the chrome-domed officer grimaced, paused a moment, then spoke directly into the cameras, saying: "The President has no intention to use force or coercion of any kind to get that stone back."

And that seemed to end it. The whole incident was widely treated as an unconventional ploy to improve America's bargaining position and settle a legitimate grievance, petulantly undermined by a Congressman talking out of turn. The news cycle moved on.

But the tweets had not quite stopped.

That evening, April 5, a Presidential tweet landed at 6:37 p.m. It read:

> Frankly, we don't need the African emerald. Bad quality. Best gems in the world are right here. But its principal. Restore American Honor!

This instantly won over Elliot Murphy, 17, of Haddonfield, New Jersey, who had just been denied use of his father's car. He had only moments earlier told the old man: "Fine. Do you think I want to be seen driving that piece of shit anyway? I just think it's bullshit. You guys treat me like shit."

Besides Elliot, the tweet appealed to many, many other Americans, including a significant portion of those who had stood in Elliot's shoes and said, or wanted to say, similar things to what he'd said to his dad.

The next evening, April 6, was a quiet one in Washington. The tweets had moved on, the press has moved on. Nothing was very exciting. Had anyone been standing on Pennsylvania Avenue, he would probably have missed the sight of a small, sprightly man being let through the service entrance at precisely 8:15 p.m. There would have been very little to see,

ODOACER

anyway. The man wore a heavy overcoat, a hat, and had an evident habit of keeping to the shadows. He stood there in the bushes one moment, and was gone the next.

One hour later, the little man reemerged, still keeping to the shadows, and hailed a taxi on Pennsylvania Avenue.

CHAPTER ONE

MONA IS ASSIGNED CLIENT-MATTER NUMBER
STIL-0024

The very famous and talented New York attorney, Vin Sinjenour, cut a debonair pose, with his feet resting on the desk and the receiver of his desk phone cradled between head and shoulder. He smiled and winked to his associate, Ms. Mona France, Esq., who sat quietly facing him as indecipherable words droned out of the receiver.

Sinjenour's 37th-floor office was bright, modern and spacious, with cream-colored walls, polished pine desktop, and a floor-to-ceiling window that almost looked out onto Times Square. Except for a small segment of shelf space dedicated to eight legal textbooks, one Blue Book, and three years' worth of annually updated state and federal rules of procedure, the walls were lined entirely with black binders, each with a client-matter number and short description printed on a slip of paper that Sinjenour's legal secretary had, with fussy regularity, affixed to the spine.

Sinjenour rolled his eyes.

"Gary, let me stop you," he said. "I know where this is going, and it's bullshit. We're *habeas*ing the shit out of this.

And, know what? The *habeas* petition will be granted. It's not even debatable. So let's not bullshit each other."

He threw his hands out toward Mona and again winked. She smiled back.

"So, one, *habeas*," Sinjenour continued. "Two, witnesses. I'm putting the dowager countess on the stand. And I think she has a very interesting story to tell. And if you try to have her excluded, I'll change venue. So fuck that, okay?"

He was now counting off on his hands. Mona scribbled along on a stenographer's pad, though all she'd written was "1. habeas corpus. 2. countess — venue???"

Sinjenour continued. His voice was confident and rather angry, if only theatrically so.

"Three, *nunc pro tunc*. Chew on that."

Mona wrote, "3. nunc?"

"And four," said Sinjenour, "We're submitting a brief on the equitable doctrine of collateral estoppel. And what are you going to say to that? No, seriously."

Mona stopped writing.

"Yeah, well," Sinjenour said after a pause, "talk to your client and call back. Tell him this isn't going to get any better for him."

The famous attorney hung up and smiled at Mona. Sinjenour had topped 40 and was rounding in the middle now; the rest — the high, rectangular forehead and tiny little mouth that barely moved when he spoke — had been with him all his life. He wore the look of someone looking for a compliment.

"What do you think?" he asked, joining words to countenance.

"It sounded good," said Mona, somewhat neutrally. In fact, some of the threats seemed to have occurred to Sinjenour on the spot, and she wasn't entirely sure she followed. But it was true that it had all *sounded* good, starting with Sinjenour's delivery and ending with the evident collapse of morale on the other end of the line.

ODOACER

In any event Sinjenour took the compliment with good grace and perhaps excessive credulity. "Yeah, and, oh, one more thing," he said. "Could you research, or have someone research, whether a *miserere mei* defense could apply in this case?"

"Sure," said Mona, jotting down a phonetic approximation of what she thought he just said.

"And — just one more thing."

Here it came. It always did.

"There's got to be a case saying that *respondeat superior* doesn't work where the employee is merely rendering feudal dues. Runs with the land or something. Could you have someone find it. Tell them not to spend too much time."

And so began another day in the life of Mona France. It began but did not end typically.

Long-suffering Mona France, the hero of our tale, was all of 30 but, short as she was, and bubbly as was her build, looked ten years younger. She had a somewhat pointy chin, short flaxen hair, and gentle grey-green eyes that lit when she smiled. She wore a conservative gray suit with a knee-length skirt and a rather fanciful black ribbon fastening her shirt collar.

This thing with the dowager countess was one of four matters she worked on with the dazzling and irascible Sinjenour, but it was all of a piece: threats, Latin, and research — typically of the variety just demanded: crazy searches for authority supporting the proposition that whatever had just entered Sinjenour's head had a unassailable basis in the common law and in equity.

Mona left the star attorney's office with a friendly goodbye — it was, after all, good to have work — and made her way to her own, somewhat smaller office, where she could instruct a hapless first-or-second year associate not to spend too much time finding support for the self-evident proposition of common sense Sinjenour just discovered, and of which she herself was now a passionate advocate.

ODOACER

Once that was done, she started drafting an affidavit, to be signed by Felix Bronstein of Bronstein Djugashvili Capital Partners LLC, in support of an arbitration petition. There simply wasn't time to bring a first-or-second-year up to speed on that.

And, perhaps between 11 and 1, she'd field a series of queries from a client that, lacking corporate counsel of its own, needed her help reviewing and rewriting the boilerplate terms of a penis pill supply contract.

After that, a break for lunch at her desk, staring at her screen some more: an online crossword puzzle, a review of the last night's episode of — too long, not enough time. The news. The focus today was for better, for worse, the President's tweets: he'd abruptly picked a fight with South Africa over —

She hadn't time for that now, either. She'd toss the remains of her lunch into the trash can in the kitchenette, so it wouldn't stink up her office, and turn to this or that brief — *mandamus*, say, or proximate causation, or, better yet, replevin — always italicize the Latin lest anyone miss the point — before hearing from the first-or-second-year his sad report that, alas, there is no legal authority in support of common sense.

She'd urge him, or her, to spend another hour or two on the matter, and suggest a few analogous situations, rooted in the brick-and-mortar world of yesteryear, that might give the associate a head start but that would, more likely, yield a half dozen opinions written before 1895, when jurists had the guts to write "it is said" and then charge directly to whatever legal proposition it was *they* were fabricating.

One thing after another, *ad infinitum*, until, if she was lucky, she'd leave around eight, feeling all the more guilty with each occupied office she passed on the way to the elevator.

But it was not to play out thusly today.

Sinjenour showed up outside Mona France's door around 2:30. She was on the phone, and so he practiced kung-

10

fu in the hall until she finished — but only when no one looked. He had deadly moves.

"You ever hear of the Chevalier Johann Peter Friedrich Ritter von Stilicho?" he asked upon being waved in.

She shook her head.

"Marquis of East Schleswig?"

No.

"The minor baron from Hammershøj?"

Still no.

"He's a famous —" Sinjenour hereupon leaned in and spoke very softly. "He's a famous international jewel thief — a client of mine. I think I've mentioned him before."

Mona thought the jewel thief part sounded familiar. Jewel theft was a relatively small part of the firm's overall practice, but Sinjenour had been developing a roster of clients in that area. Mona France shrugged and said, "oh yeah."

The one skill every legal associate learns, after all, if she is to be successful — and Mona France undoubtedly was — is knowing when she is expected to profess a certain body of knowledge about something that is completely foreign to her. There will always be time to learn whatever it is you just told someone you knew, and better that than seeming stupid.

Sinjenour continued, satisfied he'd picked the right associate for the task: "He's upstairs now, in reception. Unscheduled, but — well. Things come up. He's an important client."

Mona began writing odds and ends of what Sinjenour said to her on a fresh pad, although really there was no reason to do so.

"Anyway, I don't have time to see him. Would you go up and talk to him? Please?"

And that is where Mona France's day, and her life, became   atypical.

CHAPTER TWO

VON STILICHO REVEALS HIMSELF

By the time Mona arrived in the lobby, the receptionist had already had enough of the mysterious Chevalier Johann Peter Friedrich Ritter von Stilicho.

"Please take a seat, Mr. Stilicho," she said, firmly, nasally, to the little man leaning unacceptably far over the edge of her work station.

"Please, my dear," said the little man, "Mr. Stilicho was my father's name. Call me Ritter von Stilicho." He bestrode the reception area carelessly, pausing, from time to time, to evaluate the large pieces of 1990s kitsch art adorning the wood-paneled walls. There was considerable eye-rolling. A silent TV monitor featured a talking head babbling over the chyron "Sapphire on Fire?"

"Ritter Vaughn?" asked the receptionist.

The small man laughed gaily — "Ah! Ah-hah-hah-hah" — and clasped his hands in immense satisfaction. "As I was saying —"

Mona France cleared her throat. "Ritter von Stilicho?"

Von Stilicho spun about and, rather too studiously, took in her form.

He was a strange little man. He stood perhaps 5'6" but his posture was dignified and his movements elegant, if perhaps a bit dainty, making his height noticeable but immediately irrelevant. He wore a natty summer suit, a striking red ascot, carried under his arm a polished cane and, in the same hand — betwixt sensuous, perfectly manicured fingers — he held a straw hat with an excessively wide striped band.

He was black, but not very, with a finely sculpted van dyke and moustaches, and high, sharply arching eyebrows. The Ritter von Stilicho spoke with a clipped accent, Northern European by the sound of it, but inflected with Oxfordian cadences.

He looked Mona France up and down twice and seemingly forgot the relieved receptionist. Reaching the former in two long, bouncing strides, von Stilicho took her hand into this. "Enchanté," he pronounced, bowing low to peck a kiss on what he had taken. "I am the Chevalier Johann Peter Friedrich Peter von Stilicho, marquis of so-and-so, et cetera. And whom have I the joy of addressing?" He finally let go her hand when Mona yanked it away with a subtle but unmistakable tug.

"Ritter von—"

"Please," the aristocrat said, "call be Johann Peter. Or Hanno."

"Chevalier," said Mona, brokering no dissent, "my name is Mona France. I work with Vin Sinjenour."

The Chevalier raised an eyebrow and smiled warmly. "Yes, yes, the great jurist himself. Did I not see on the website he was in 'Super Lawyers'?"

"Yes," replied Mona, "something like that. Anyhow, he — Vin — sends his regrets. He is unavailable at the moment. He asked that I talk to you about your—"

She really didn't know why he was here. "About your matter," she said finally.

ODOACER

The small man's expression darkened, and his tone, previously so light and gay, lowered into something almost conspiratorial. "Yes," he said at last. "My matter as you say." He looked furtively toward the receptionist with an expression that was anything but trusting. "I think we should discuss that in private."

Mona exhaled. "Yes, Chevalier," she said. "I can get us a conference room."

But he would have none of that. He once again took on the mask — was it a mask? — of a carefree gadabout. "Oh, no, lovely Mona —"

"Please, Chevalier, you flatter me, but Mona is sufficient."

"Lovely! Ah? Ah! Ah-hah-hah-hah!" he laughed gaily. "Mona, as I was saying, no, a conference room is simply out of the question. I know a spot in a park, the one not far from here — the *Central* Park. You are familiar? Of course, yes, it is well known. We shall have a picnic!"

Having never fielded such an offer, Mona France had too little time to formulate a convincing refusal. And so she agreed to accompany the Chevalier to Central Park for a charmingly   conspiratorial   picnic.

14

CHAPTER THREE

CHARLES DECIDES TO VISIT DINERS

Charles Earl Jarlesberg III, aged 41 years, stopped running as he passed his building's back gate, then halted the exercise tracker on his watch. It had been, as it had always been, 2.67 miles around the park — a feat he had accomplished in a not impressive 27.45 minutes. Breathing heavily, but with the feeling of floating, he strolled down to the Marsh — a small, well-kept public easement by the boathouse that bordered a tidal mudflat. It was low tide and a cold, drizzly, early spring day.

He was here today, like he was every other day, to cool down and think after his run. But he was also here today for a meeting. He had been running a lot lately and thinking a lot lately, and he had decided he needed to do something. Before he could do this thing, he needed to consult with an advisor — a very trusted, very special advisor.

Charles looked like — *you*. Except, to the extent you are not white, male, a bit heavy, and in your forties, he was a bit more of those things. Otherwise, you.

Charles Earl Jarlsberg III, finding the pier empty, found a spot, leaned against the rail, and watched the little

15

rivulets coursing their way through the mud, only to be overtaken, now and then, by the opposite and overwhelming force of a passing boat's wake. On and on it went.

This little scene could, of course, have been construed as a ham-fisted and not especially original metaphor for futility — or, more hopefully, but no less tiredly, it could inspire musings on borrowed time and the limited nature of human achievement, the gratitude we must feel for — whatever, and what not — but Charles Earl Jarlsberg III was not in a metaphorical mood. He was not, in fact, in any way, a metaphorical man. He was a man of deep thoughts, perhaps, but he was also a man of action, of great, startling action.

Charles Earl Jarlsberg III was, or course, a great captain of the RESISTANCE: that force which had coalesced in the aftermath of the current President's election to carry the torch for — the last President, certainly, but also for a certain idea of America that, perhaps, is more convincingly felt than it is described. You know.

Charles Earl Jarlsberg III was in the fight to make that certain idea real. He had done so much to make it so. He had an email list. He organized post-card writing parties at bars. He went to meetings, sometimes two, three, or even four before the particular group sponsoring them sputtered out. He went to marches, organized buses. Signed online petitions, called Congressional offices. He sat on a bench by the farmer's market on Saturdays and proclaimed, loudly and with conviction and logic, his refusal to accept as legitimate the carnival of cruelty that had sprung up around them.

But as he stood on that pier on that cold spring day, watching those very literal little rivulets find their way, imperfectly, to the river, he thought:

I must go to them!

It was the first thing he heard in the morning, the last thing he heard at night. Not really the words — for thought isn't experienced that way, except when thought about — but the ideas. The five words, or one thought, came to him

ODOACER

unwelcome, overstayed whatever welcome it had, and interrupted happier trains of thought: I must go to them.

And this them was the Red Hats.

Charles had become convinced there was a deep and game-changing truth about America to be unlocked in their diners. Or, if not in their diners, in their church basements. Or, if not there, in their barbershops, bleachers or bars. Charles Earl Jarlsberg III had read about in the *Times*, and elsewhere, and needed to see for himself, all the odd ones, the unexpected and counterintuitive things: the voter who voted for this guy and then that guy — the voter who voted for another guy and then this guy — the voter whose votes in three consecutive elections in some way did not tell a very neat story — the one who liked rap but voted for — who listed to jazz and — the place where the plant closed — where they all love the Mexican place but — but but but.

He would go to the Red Hats and discover the deep, soulful counterintuitive truths that, the *Times* promised, lay hidden in wait — and then! He would, Charles, the Resistor, would carefully, gradually, and ever so skillfully teach them: Their True Interests.

These were hidden from them. These were shrouded in false consciousness. The Red Hats were cut off, by some devilish trick, from the base of material economic relations that, alone, represented both the origin of human cognition and the future of human aspiration. That was why they engaged in all manner of irreconcilable thought and behavior: voting for this guy then that guy listening to rap working in the plant eating Mexican et cetera. Their universe of associations was unglued. But they could be saved. So sure of this was Charles Earl Jarlsberg III that he would make it his mission now to do so.

But before he went to see these things, and to have his epiphany about America, and before he could rescue the Red Hats from debilitating blindness to Their True Interests, he needed advice.

Charles Earl Jarlsberg III checked his watch.

17

ODOACER

3:36.

He would arrive any minute.

"Charles Earl Jarlsberg," went a lilting voice behind him. Charles turned and found his gaze drawn down, slightly and magnetically, toward the short, sprightly, athletic form of Hanno. He wore a beige summer suit, though it was still spring, and a very wide striped tie, knotted — as Hanno's ties always were — jauntily. The little man smiled broadly, exposing fine rows of tiny white teeth. He strode to Charles' side and, assuming his friend's thoughtful pose prior to the interruption, leaned on the rail of the pier. Charles Earl Jarlsberg III leaned next to him.

"Fine day," said Hanno, "it is a very, very — fine — day." He said *fine* with stilted emphasis, as though trying to translate some native term that didn't quite find an equivalent in English but that, in its native iteration, conveyed a profound and resonant "fine." He nodded, ever so subtly, to what appeared to be an old woman seated two benches down from them. Charles Earl Jarlsberg III understood.

"Yes," he said. "I was just admiring the geese."

A goose family had ventured onto the mudflat, mom and dad goose standing anxious sentry while the two babies waddled carelessly about the muck in search of whatever filth they ate.

"Yes, the geese," repeated Hanno. "I believe Canada Geese they are called, yes? They have made good on that old vow. Eh? Ah? Ah-hah-hah-ha!" He laughed gaily. "And yet, they have come back."

Charles Earl Jarlsberg III frowned, but his sour mood had no obvious effect on Hanno, who tittered on at his own lame little jests. He continued on about Canada, and geese, and then other kinds of birds, and the countries they were named after, and how usually the country's name took on an adjectival form in such instances. He had been going on in this manner for entirely too long when, finding a suitable pause, Charles spoke up. Nodding at the animals, he said, "there were three babies last week."

ODOACER

Hanno looked at the birds, showing just a pang of concern, and shrugged. "Yes, well." he said. "I suppose it must be that way, no. If they all survived we'd be overrun by geese, wouldn't we. And yet," he smiled sadly, "I can't imagine mother and father goose look at it that way."

"No," said Charles. "I suppose not."

"Well!" said Hanno.

"Well," Charles repeated. "They hiss at you. If you get too close to them."

"The birds?"

"Yes. The parents. They go" — and he made a sound from the roof of his mouth — "huh-uh-uh-gh!"

"Huh-uh-uh-gh!" repeated Hanno with a mischievous giggle. "Yes, quite scary. Scary indeed."

"It is. It is in fact."

Hanno fell silent. Neither spoke for a minute as the tragic bird family waddled off through the filth. Hanno, Charles, goose mom and goose dad all watched with trepidation as a flock of some five or six adults, still smaller than the parents, alit at the water's edge.

"Those guys," muttered the literal Charles with a wry smile.

"Those guys?"

"I imagine them the young dudes. No kids, no worries."

"Are they all boys?" Hanno was craning his head, as though by doing so he'd be able to get a look at the birds' undersides and, by doing that, be able to discern their sexes.

"I don't know," was the un-metaphorical answer. "I just think of them that way. They think they're. But, you know, but. They're actually pathetic. If they were us, they'd be waiting in line for brunch."

"Uh-huh." Hanno nodded.

Again, a silence, while the birds went about their business. The youngbloods paid no mind to the family.

"I wonder why they hiss," said Charles, at last.

"To protect their babies."

19

"Yes, but. Why do they hiss at me? If it's a hawk they're afraid of." He nodded toward the wooded hill and the steep cliffs across the river. "If it's a hawk they're afraid of, doesn't it help to shelter under? A big ape?"

Hanno smiled, shrugged, didn't answer. "Fine animals. Fine."

"Like birds in nature documentaries," continued Charles. "On buffalos. It seems safe."

The small man in the summer suit and too-broad tie straightened. His voice became only just discernibly sharper, but carried with it infinite authority. "The parents do not look at it that way."

"They don't understand."

"Perhaps. In any event, they won't change."

Charles Earl Jarlsberg III exhaled heavily.

"Well," he said. "Thank you for coming. It's been — worthwhile." Charles was not a metaphorical person, as you have been told, so whatever he got from this oblique conversation must be left to the imagination.

Hanno smiled sharply, lay a perfectly-manicured hand sympathetically on Charles' shoulder. "So — you are going?"

"Yes. I must."

The little man reached into an interior pocket and took from it a small manilla envelope, sealed. He handed it to his friend.

"Then go with God," he said. "But, even with Him, be very, very careful."

CHAPTER FOUR

THEY VISIT THE CENTRAL PARK

Somehow the Chevalier Johann Peter Friedrich Peter von Stilicho had managed to change in the interval between his taking leave of Mona at the firm and meeting her in the Central Park, just opposite the Plaza. He wore a top hat, garish maroon cumber-bun, and a heavy black mantle that seemed ill-suited to the cool but not cold spring weather.

"Ah, Mona France!" he exclaimed, and bowed deeply when she failed to offer a hand to kiss. "Please, come with me. Jørgen has been hard at work." He pronounced the last name as it is meant to be pronounced: yeh-err-N.

Von Stilicho led her up a long footpath along the pond and then past the ice skating rink, closed for the season. He stood irritatingly close as they walked, leaning in, almost until his lips pressed Mona's ear, to offer little anecdotes about New York's elite — different members of which evidently leapt to mind at each footbridge, statue, or playground. Mona tried to follow the names but, to the extent she recognized any of them, she was quite sure the targets of the Chevalier's mean-spirited jests had been dead for decades.

ODOACER

She laughed nonetheless, though without much mirth, and she had to be positively firm when, on more than one occasion, the chevalier took her hand in an illustrative or merely affectionate gesture and then failed to let go.

At last they arrived in the secluded grove which was their initial destination.

There, standing under a tree, besides a pile of picnic baskets, blankets, and assorted knick-knacks, was a tall, dour man in dark culottes, dark frock coat and a gray powdered wig. His stockings were slightly worn. He had a broad, downturned mouth, and looked to be about 60.

"This is Jørgen," exclaimed the Chevalier with a merry wave of the hand. "Jørgen is my taciturn butler. And how are we today, Jørgen?"

Taciturn Jørgen lowered his eyes. A bow, or a nod of the head, would have been too ostentatious a response.

"Very good, Jørgen. Very good. Well!" The Chevalier scanned the environs. "I'd picked out a spot a bit up the path. Come, Mona France."

He held out his hand, which she did not take, and, unaffected by the rebuff, skipped merrily up the path. Mona walked behind, saying little, and sneaking the occasional peek at taciturn Jørgen, who had loaded the huge pile of picnic baskets, blankets, and assorted knick-knacks on his back and, hunched under the load, silently, long-sufferingly, heaved it up the hill.

They arrived at a secluded patch of grass in the part of the park identified on maps as Cedar Hill. While the Chevalier lounged on a blanket — one leg along the ground, the other bowed, torso twisted, head resting in elegant, perfectly manicured fingers, taciturn Jørgen set about preparing the picnic. Jørgen made sure that the lounging Chevalier and Mona France, who sat on the ground, arms crossed, had suitable aperitifs and continued his intricate, wordless preparations while his master offered up the broad strokes of his autobiography to a woman who was preoccupied with her work and, it must be said, wasn't terribly interested.

ODOACER

The Chevalier described himself variously as a raconteur, a boulevardier, a roué, and a confirmed scapegrace and scourge of civility such that Mona — with an attorney's acquired preference for defined terms used repeatedly and unvaryingly — could hardly keep straight his many masks. She decided though, as the details droned on about her at the level of passing consciousness, that these were hardly mutually exclusive categories and all very likely fitting for a man of the Chevalier's profession and reputation.

He came from Denmark or northern Germany. Or had grown up there. It was suggested he'd been adopted from Saint-Domingue, as he called it. But his temperament and sympathies were in all respects very much those of aristocracy tempered by decades of social democracy. He had a smug self-confidence and an easy sense of superiority, which had evidently reached its apotheosis in his superior ability to hold forth with, and relate to, people of commoner disposition. Clearly no stranger to slumming, or to bragging about it, he had more to say about ports, port dwellers, and port brothels than Mona cared to hear. Yet she nodded along and asked the occasional question, if only for the sake of fostering happy attorney-client relations. From the brothels to this or that literary *demimonde* — the Chevalier's word — and the next attempt to conceal her flagging interest.

For a man of, perhaps, forty-five, he had surprisingly vivid opinions on the outcome of the Second Schleswig War, though he made emphatically clear that his family's holdings had been kept intact on both sides of the "new" border. Of course, he recounted with a certain wistfulness, it was not "the modern way" to hold them through the subsequent tumult, and the assets had been diversified, decidedly away from northern European agricultural real estate. The Nazis made their appearance, as one supposes they must, and the aristocrat made clear that "we" — Mona assumed he meant his family, although that wasn't clear — had enthusiastically allowed the Danish Resistance to collect airdrops on their estates, and listened to Allied radio whenever the opportunity permitted.

ODOACER

And had, perhaps, a black sheep uncle been led astray? Had an aunt's dullard husband made mistakes? Well, such things are unfortunate. But they are salvaged, to a degree, by those four wonderful words, beautiful in any language, "only in the *wehrmacht.*"

And so on.

Taciturn Jørgen had finished setting up the picnic, and now stood at attention off to the side a bit. The raconteur had recounted much — he'd barely stopped talking a moment — but hadn't said a word about how Mona or her firm could be of service.

"Ah!" he exclaimed at last. "Our picnic is ready."

There were lawn chairs, and a table, and a little awning to keep the mist off. There were blankets on which rested baskets of shiny fruit, cutting boards heaped with cheeses, and bowls of small Baltic shrimp. And there was, a few paces up the hill, a little tent: a romantic interpretation of what one might find at a medieval tournament, complete with red and white stripes and a little banner flapping on top.

The Chevalier nodded to this and winked at Mona. "For later," he said. "Should we find ourselves in the mood for some privacy."

Mona grimaced. "I'm quite certain, Chevalier Ritter von Stilicho, that this picnic will be conducted professionally."

The Chevalier mirrored her frown, although there was something ironic, even jesting, in his expression.

He caught Jørgen's eye, noted the taciturn man's raised eyebrow, and mouthed — in fact whispered, loud enough for Mona to hear — "leave it for now."

Mona took a lawn chair, and in doing so moved a few paces further from the Chevalier.

Lunch, the actual eating of it, passed mostly in silence. Jørgen, clearly, was not about to light up the moment; Mona squirmed awkwardly while eating the small Baltic shrimp; and the Chevalier seemed to have lost his interest in talking.

Mona looked at her watch. Two hours had passed. She assumed this time was billable, but still couldn't believe how much of her day had been wasted on the decline of northern Europe's nobility. "Chevalier," she said after a particularly uneventful five minutes.

The Chevalier had been lying on a blanket, watching the leaves dance in the breeze, but now sat up with a dopey smile. He did not answer.

"Chevalier," said Mona again, meaning to turn to the matter of business.

He shushed her with a downturned hand. He was transfixed by something he saw along the footpath. A matron, a proper Upper East Side Matron, perhaps sixty, sharply dressed, and having had some work done, perhaps, walking a large Afghan hound.

"Egad what a magnificent specimen," exclaimed the Chevalier upon seeing the beast. He hunched behind a downed tree trunk and observed, urging by his hand gestures that Mona — who had, instinctively, assumed a like posture — keep quiet.

"Taciturn Jørgen," he whispered. He made another gesture, one which the taciturn butler evidently understood, for the latter removed from the campsite one of two hunting rifles that had been propped against an old tulip tree and, with little fanfare, presented this to the Chevalier. It was a long, immaculately polished affair, with a heavy wood butt intricately carved with curlycue patterns and monogrammed initials that did not appear to be the Chevalier's.

Silently, the Chevalier loaded the gun at its breech, lay down snugly behind the old trunk, and took aim at the hound. "I must have it for my collection," he whispered to Mona. "For science!"

"Are you fucking crazy?" shouted Mona, giving the barrel a shove.

The matron, who had been oblivious to all goings on, took a quick look at the Chevalier, Mona, taciturn Jørgen, and the gun, and, with her hound, beat a hasty retreat down the path.

"My darling," said the Chevalier, matter-of-factly, "you ruined my shot."

Then he laughed gaily. "Ah? Ah! A-hah-hah!"

Mona did not.

"Chevalier," she implored him, as he handed the rifle back to taciturn Jørgen, "can we please discuss why you have asked for this meeting? What do you need from us?"

"Yes," said the Chevalier, turning serious again. "That. Shall we discuss it in the tent?"

"No, Chevalier. Not in the tent! Let's discuss it here. Or back at the firm, in a conference room."

The little man shrugged.

"Very well," he said. He looked about cursorily and, evidently finding nothing suspicious, gave the following report in a matter-of-fact, not especially quiet or conspiratorial tone of voice: "I have been retained by the President of the United States to steal the Cape Town Sapphire and give it to him. As you know, I am an international jewel thief. I have accepted the assignment. The Sapphire will be stolen and delivered. But I wish to take out a certain — how do you say? — insurance policy. For myself and, more importantly, for the world. That is to say, I wish to have the details of this engagement documented in a thorough, and, let us say, legally sufficient manner — one that could, if necessary, satisfy rules of evidence, et cetera."

"Chevalier!" gasped Mona, astonished. "Do you mean to blackmail the President?"

"No!" protested the chevalier with a terse, but not altogether gay, laugh. "No. I merely wish for the President to know that I know what I know. And for him to know that I know he knows this. Do you see?"

"And what do you mean to do with this —" Mona paused, searched for the right word. "With this advantage?"

The Chevalier's countenance darkened again. He raised an eyebrow and looked deeply into the attorney's — or, as he would have said, the "young female attorney's" — eyes.

ODOACER

"I mean to ensure world peace for the balance of the President's term," he said grimly. "And I need you, Mona France, to help me."

CHAPTER FIVE

THE SEKSHAUS FAMILY VACATION

Mona France still was not exactly sure how she, and her firm, fit into the Chevalier's rather grandiose plan to blackmail — but not really blackmail — the putative leader of the free world into thirty-one months of relatively good behavior. But she knew he was a client in need of legal services, or of services a lawyer was arguably competent to provide. And when she had mentioned the scheme, or what she understood of it, to her visionary boss and mentor, the famous Vin Sinjenour, he was understanding.

"Yes," he had said, stroking his jutting, manly jaw. "This is a very unusual assignment, to be sure, and not necessarily one we'll be able to include in our marketing literature. But —" and here he gestured toward some unseen being in the sky, or thereabouts, "the LAW" — he certainly said this word as though intending it to be fully capitalized in the transcription — and also as though intending it would someday be transcribed — "the LAW," he said again, "does not answer to our petty needs."

Mona had found this mystifying, just as she found Sinjenour's subsequent exegesis on the common law — which

ODOACER

he held was embedded in the firmament of the universe and discoverable through the agency of REASON (also capitalized) — mystifying. All the more so because everything the Chevalier intended, and in which she, Sinjenour and the firm would be complicit, was of highly dubious legality. But she expected the far-seeing Sinjenour had in mind a greater good, the LAW as in the RULE OF LAW, which he'd undoubtedly have wanted capitalized, and perhaps also international law, or some other more practical, less metaphysically exalted kind of law not requiring capitalization, that appeared threatened by the current inclement circumstances.

And so arrangements had been made for other associates to take on her other assignments, at least for the period the Chevalier needed her. An expense account was set up and Mona was provided a direct line to the firm's travel agent.

Needless to say, neither this logistical planning, nor a set of nervous goodbyes in his own office, nor the many emails Mona sent to her colleagues warning of her impending absence, would have or could have been missed by the observant eye of the great Sinjenour. He had told her, more than once, not to worry, even a little bit, about other matters, and to concentrate only on the important task at hand, and he expressly forbade her colleagues to contact her on business during the pendency of the scheme. But none of this would stop him from sending Mona many, many unanswered work emails in the weeks that would follow. Or from getting vaguely irritated when he remembered, belatedly, that he had whimsically given away his most trusted associate to a dubious nobleman planning to defraud the government.

But Mona would know little of that. She had a job to do.

And so here she was, in the grand entrance of the American Museum of Natural History, beneath the fighting dinosaur skeletons, wearing what the Chevalier had referred to as "a widow outfit, but sexy" — consisting of a short black dress and a short black veil over her eyes — and pushing the Chevalier in a wheelchair.

He had assigned to Mona the role of grieving trophy wife and taken for himself the role of invalid adult son (his term, not Mona's).

Unsaid was why they needed to pose as the closest survivors of one Justus Sekshaus, or why their supposed connection to the late Justus Sekshaus — whose backstory was rather sketchily drawn — got them any closer to Cape Town Sapphire. Or why they needed disguises at all. But the Chevalier had insisted.

"You might ask yourself, my dear," he had said with unusual peevishness as they prepared for this "infiltration" in his midtown suites, "who, of the two of us, is the international jewel thief?"

And so they wore disguises.

The late Mr. Sekshaus was evidently not a museum member, or in any event had not purchased a family membership, and his son, perhaps an ill fit for this world in many respects, had the wherewithal to draw the distinction between a suggested donation and an admission fee. Feet stomped. Red-faced, Mona had put a stop to this, paying the full donation on the firm's expense account and, in addition, buying tickets to the butterfly exhibit that she didn't really intend to use.

"My word," whispered the Chevalier as Mona pushed him past the African mammals, "I despise butterflies. I won't permit it. I won't."

"Just be cool, Ritter von Stilicho," Mona said, half intending to deposit him in the butterfly room after all.

"To the Hall of Gems," the Chevalier sputtered.

"I know."

The museum was not too crowded. It was still early spring, a weekday, still early in the morning, and the weather was nice. But it must have been a spring break somewhere in Germany, for the Teutons were out in force, their clean, tall teenagers more politely indulgent of their parents than were their American counterparts on vacation in the big city.

"Half these people are probably Sekshauses," Mona grumbled.

"Good, we'll fit right in."

"Are we supposed to be German?"

"German-American," said the Chevalier.

"You could have told me that."

"You're doing perfect. Don't change anything."

And so it proceeded as they made their way to the centerpiece of the Hall of Gems, the Cape Town Sapphire, on loan from the South African government as — the reader shall be reminded — a symbolic coda to the gem's contentious history.

It looked exactly what one would expect a famous sapphire to look like. It was big, glassy, and glistening, faintly-colored green. It was encased in glass, and the glass case lay four or five feet behind a rope, and the rope was flanked by security guards.

The Chevalier took a furtive look around, then pointed, ever-so-subtly, with his elegant, perfectly-manicured finger, to a series of red dots positioned about the room. "Lasers," he whispered to Mona.

She nodded. She really had very little idea for how to go about what the Chevalier intended to do.

"Pictures," he whispered.

Mona removed a small, obsolete digital camera from her purse and took a few shots — of the gem, or the security, or the Chevalier in front of all these things. This they had planned in advance. It was part of the Chevalier's altogether dubious plan for "legal documentation" of the heist. "Say cheese, Ferdinand."

The Chevalier made an embarrassing squawk that, Mona assumed, was Ferdinand saying cheese. She decided she would make no such requests of Ferdinand going forward.

But she got the shot.

ODOACER

"Very good, my dear," the Chevalier whispered when she had finished. "Now we must find a way to take the Sapphire."

Mona again surveyed the room. The guards weren't armed, but they had radios, and in addition to the case and the lasers, the two exits appeared to have some kind of fortified steel doors implanted in the bulkheads. She guessed these would seal if anyone made a play for the sapphire.

"I have no idea," Mona said.

"Tut tut." Von Stilicho irritatingly placed a hand on her arm. "Leave that to me. I need only —" he paused.

A tour group had entered the chamber — mostly Germans — led by a docent, a squat, heavily made up woman with a amber necklace and a loose-fitting sweater. Her name was Miriam Roth. Her accent carried the sonorous intonations of the long island to their east.

"And here is the centerpiece of our temporary collection, the famed Cape Town Sapphire," she said.

The Chevalier seemed lost in wonderment. His eyes drank in the form of Miriam Roth. With a flicker of the tongue, the tip only, really, but it was perceptible, he wet his lips. At last he finished his earlier thought: "I need only inspiration," he said, trailing off.

"Inspiration," hissed Mona. "Inspiration for what?"

The Chevalier turned to look at her. His expression was not that of Ferdinand Sekshaus, non-verbal invalid son and heir of the late Justus Sekshaus. His expression was that of a different kind of man completely.

"Inspiration," he repeated, throatily, curling his lips, "for seduction!"

CHAPTER SIX

SCENES FROM A DINER

It looked in all respects like a diner ought: long windows along the front, a polished aluminum facade, and a raised entrance with a little foyer wherein, Charles Earl Jarlsberg III would presently confirm, "car shopper" brochures and real estate ads were to be had.

Inside, it was not exactly bustling, but the booths were mostly full, as well as the stools bounding the long Formica counter. The seats were upholstered in a somewhat worn maroon leatherette, and the shelving along the back wall was of a gray wood-grain synthetic. The patrons chatted quietly or, if they were alone, scanned local newspapers or their devices. They were older, most of them, and on the whole white. Many of the men wore caps with high, starchy panels advertising the names of teams, auto parts retailers, national parks, and the like. Clothes were ironed, and patterned, button-up shirts were neatly tucked into light slacks. At a couple tables lounged dingier patrons, these dressed in jeans, cover-alls, Carhartt jackets and the like, evidently heading to or coming from shifts.

ODOACER

After exchanging brief words with the hostess — a large, sleepy-eyed woman with big, sculpted hair and a mole above her lip — and who took an unsubtle liking, by the way, to some aspect of his appearance that is also an aspect of your appearance — Charles took a seat at the counter. He ordered a coffee from the hispanic server.

Hammer News played almost mutely on a small, vacuum-tube-style television mounted above the service window. It was a panel show. The chyron read: "Healthcare Crisis."

"Would you turn it up?" came a husky voice originating two seats over and addressing the hispanic server. There was a hint of challenge in the voice, almost as though the hispanic server had just turned down the sound. But, given that this was evidently a panel discussion about health care rather than border security, Charles chalked this up to the regional cadences. All this he thought in the time it took for him to zero in on the speaker.

It was a tall, younger man, perhaps in his early 30s, with dark, neatly-groomed hair and a Brooks Brothers shirt. He seemed to be finishing a very light breakfast consisting of toast and some peeled fruit.

Charles nodded politely to this man, and the nod was returned.

The sound went up.

In the inset, a slight, soft-spoken man with glasses was trying to make a point about health care while the panelists, all dressed and groomed as though they worked in the regional sales office of the same car parts manufacturers advertised on the hats, and practiced in the art of casual cruelty, stared in disbelief. The man trying to talk was a liberal academic of second- or third-rate stature who, it would become evident, abased himself by serving as the panel's designated punching bag. He was the kind of person who, upon being cut off mid-sentence, would nod along, grinning smugly, until his interrupter had said his piece — as though wishing to make an ostentatious display of patience, but really only displaying his

ODOACER

own spinelessness. The whole debate was a highly ritualized affair.

"You simply cannot have coverage," the doormat said, blowing up to full-screen while the panel took to the inset, "cheaply, for everyone, regardless of condition, if healthy people are not paying into the system. And guess what?" He was employing a gruesomely ineffective common touch. "Healthy people get sick. So it's fair. It's fair to have the individual mandate, and —"

"Wait a minute," interrupted one of the panelists, a fifty-year-old man with gray hair and ever-furrowing eyebrows, "telling people to buy health insurance — the government telling you and me to buy health insurance. That's supposed to be fair now?"

"And look," interjected another panelist, a slightly puffy man in his forties with dark, curly hair, cut short, "Look," he repeated while the liberal academic stewed in his inset, still nodding stupidly in the spirit of informed debate, "this system, this health law, is in free fall, okay? And it's in free fall, frankly, because people hate this law. Let's look at the numbers."

Some numbers popped up on the screen, along with a new chyron. They didn't seem to tell any story, but the man with the dark hair was telling a story about a health law in free fall and there were numbers on the screen. The liberal academic nodded and even squinted a bit, following his opponent's take very carefully right up to the moment the gray-haired panelist announced they'd have to go commercial and had another guest lined up for when they came back with a fun human interest story.

"Fuck," said the young man two seats down as they in fact went to commercial. "Fucking socialists," he said to no one in particular, though obviously meaning, on some buried level, both the enactors of the health law in free fall, the punching bag, and the hispanic server. This man, thought Charles with a start, does not understand His True Interests.

ODOACER

And then there was a buzz. In the pocket of Charles Earl Jarlsberg III, and coming from the man's device, which had been laid out on the counter next to his fruit bowl. After the buzz, each took a look.

It was a tweet from the President of the United States, popping up in both their alerts:

The health law, it said, was (the Tweet didn't use the verb, skipping directly to the characterization) "incredibly unpopular, and now failing very badly because of individual mandate. Government should not tell people to buy health insurance."

The next tweet came ten seconds later:

We will make a new and better law that will cover pre-existing conditions without violating sacred individual rights under Constitution. Health care should be available to all, but NO SOCIALISM!

"How can anyone even argue with this?" muttered the man, evidently wanting to be heard. "The data doesn't lie."

BUZZ, came the third and final tweet of the episode. "Numbers tell the story," it said. "#Freefall!" below that was a screenshot from the recently-ended segment, showing the numbers that had just been thrown up to silence the hapless nodding liberal academic.

Charles Earl Jarlsberg III drew a deep breath. It was now or never.

"By god," he exclaimed, loudly, silencing most of those around him as he brought a fist crashing down on the table, "the President is right!"

The young man looked quizzically at this new and strange person — as though what he'd said was right but hadn't come out right. Nonetheless, as the ordinary hum of the diner revived, he paid Charles the courtesies of a grim smile and a slight nod. Then he paid his bill and left, pulling on as he went out a red trucker's cap bearing the familiar slogan.

36

ODOACER

It had happened.

Charles Earl Jarlsberg III had made contact with a Red Hat.

CHAPTER SEVEN

THE ART OF SEDUCTION

The Chevalier had learned — never mind how — that the enigmatic Miriam Roth was meeting her docent friends at a Starbucks this evening at seven. Mona had been assured, but not convinced, that von Stilicho's meeting her, Miriam, there, Starbucks, would pave the way to grand larceny and beyond that to Presidential blackmail and who knew what else and, moreover, that she should come along. So come along she did, keeping up with but not quite walking beside the odd little nobleman as he bounded up Columbus Avenue.

He gesticulated widely to the sky. "I knew it!" he exclaimed. "I knew that a woman of Miriam Roth's temperament would be drawn, irresistibly pulled, to the languid allures of the coffee house!"

The Chevalier wore jodhpurs, a poofy-sleeved shirt, and a fussy little vest, bound tight about the waste. The outfit matched the humid, heavy dusk through which he so energetically sliced. His mood was ebullient.

"A touch risqué?" he continued, ostensibly addressing Mona. "Yes, that is Miriam! Oh god! Coffee houses are places for scoundrels. But, also, the natural habitat of the

ODOACER

artist, the intellectual, the reactionary, the bomb-thrower — sometimes all that in one package. And more."

He paused and waited for Mona, who reluctantly allowed herself to catch up. "You must be careful," he whispered, resting an elegant, perfectly-manicured hand on her forearm. "Of the dizzying drug — yes. More, even more so, of the ideas. Dangerous ideas, Mona France. Dangerous and lovely and pregnant with beauty and terror and lust!"

And so he went on until, at last, they arrived at the glass-paned door of the neighborhood Starbucks and, with one final admonition to resist the siren call of whatever hedonistic anarcho-syndicalist puritanism lay in wait, entered.

"Behold," whispered the Chevalier hoarsely, "the secret *demimonde*" — assuredly meant to be italicized — "of the coffee house."

It did, in fact, look different from what Mona had expected.

The wait staff wore fezes and pantaloons, and brought little cups of very bitter coffee to the tables on silver trays. A band sat in a haze of fragrant smoke, plucking two-and-three stringed instruments along a decidedly non-Western scale. And the clientele appeared a combination of gentlemen and women of leisure, artists, lovers — or so Mona was informed, she could not see what gave them away — confirmed cutthroats, and city politicians.

"Ah!" exclaimed the Chevalier, "it is his excellency the mayor."

To Mona's great shock, it was in fact the mayor, towering and dapper, a longish cigarette holder clenched betwixt his somewhat horsy teeth. The Chevalier took her by the hand to the awaiting grandee and introduced her. "Mr. Mayor, my old friend, I wish to introduce you to my companion — perhaps — I hope — Ms. Mona France."

Mona offered the mayor her hand. "It is a pleasure, Ms. France," said the mayor. "Hanno has told me so much about you."

39

ODOACER

Mona was not sure when and how so much information could have been conveyed to the mayor, and certainly not of what to say, so she smiled stupidly and nodded.

The mayor laughed heartily and told a charming anecdote about a recent quarrel with the comptroller that had ended, by an improbable chain of causation, with the public advocate seated backward on an old donkey, "singing like a drunk Irishman." All laughed, even Mona, and especially the Chevalier, who of course laughed gaily. And yet, amidst the revelry, as Mona paired off in conversation with the famed author of *Foul Wonderful War!*, who dressed very much like he'd just that moment returned from a rather long yachting trip, the Chevalier became deadly serious. Mona, through the corner of her eye, watched him lean into the Mayor's ear — actually, the much taller mayor did the leaning, but the effect was similar — and she heard him whisper, "Mr. Mayor, I shall need a moment of your time."

And, as the author of *Foul Wonderful War!* recounted a very wittily told episode about Melanesian headhunters, Mona watched, with growing concern, as the two men sulked off to the shadows, grim-faced, to talk about who knew what.

And, yet, when the Chevalier returned a few moments later, he was the picture of carefree *joie de vivre*. "And now, Mona," he said, "I must do what I came here to do."

"Which is?"

Mona took a long, wolfish look in the direction of Miriam Roth. "Seduce!" he said.

With that he took leave of the young female attorney, surrendering her to the creepily escalating attentions of the author of *Foul Wonderful War!*, and sauntered to the table of Miriam Roth and her raucous docent friends.

Through a series of noncommittal responses, evasions, and excuses to the author's manifold requests and then pleadings, Mona watched.

The Chevalier started a conversation. Miriam Roth smiled. The conversation continued. She smiled more. And,

ODOACER

like that, Miriam Roth left Starbucks at the side of the Chevalier Johann Peter Friedrich Ritter von Stilicho.

Mona France returned to the hotel suites she shared with the Chevalier, showered, and went to bed.

CHAPTER EIGHT

THE DINER YIELDS ITS SECRET

Charles Earl Jarlsberg III had returned to the diner every day, at the same time, for six days after his lucky encounter with the Red Hat who did not understand His Own Interests. On the seventh he rested, the diner being closed for the Sabbath, and on the eighth he again got lucky.

The man arrived a few minutes after he did and assumed the seat directly next to Charles. "Morning," he said with a nod before losing himself in his phone. He did not seem to be looking at anything in particular, just avoiding conversation before its time had come.

"Morning," said Charles.

The man ordered, stared at his phone, grumbled something indistinct about a hockey team, was served, gulped an orange juice, sent a text message, scanned the headlines, and at length put down his phone. "What's on this morning?" He said, plainly addressing Charles. He jerked his head in the direction of the TV set. It was the same Hammer News panel, muted. The chyron read: "FBI Out of Control: Bombshell Report."

ODOACER

Charles sighed with what he hoped approximated extreme exasperation.

"God damn investigation."

The man rolled his eyes. "Hey," he said, as the hispanic server scampered by, "could you turn it up?" This was done. When it was, the man said "Ken," and offered Charles Earl Jarlsberg III his hand.

Charles took it. "Charles," he said.

Ken was already watching the panel show. Charles did as he did. A Congressman was explaining something to the panel.

" . . . and what we're finding," he said, "is really amazing. It is clear to me, Ron, from these latest revelations, that the FBI team investigating the campaign got its marching orders from someone the White House. And its mission was clear as can be: get the campaign. By any means."

"F'wut your saying is true," interjected the gray-haired host, evidently Ron, who didn't see fit to fully voice the word "if" on these occasions, "this is a massive, shocking, Watergate-level violation of civil rights . . ."

"Fucking unbelievable," Ken said. "These fucking people" — that is, apparently, unspecified members of the previous administration — "should be in jail. Or worse, right?"

Charles nodded. Their phones buzzed.

It was the President.

Unbelievable Watergate level corruption in prior White House. Ordered FBI to spy on my campaign for political purposes. Perpetrators will be investigated and punished with prison or worse. Civil Right!

"That's what I said!" exclaimed the triumphant Ken. "Unbelievable!"

"Nice." Charles offered the man a smile — making it suitably, self-consciously grim. They were discussing profound things after all.

The panel was still at it with the Congressman, a mean-looking character from Florida with a bulldog face framed by a slapdash haircut. The gist of his bombshell information was that a White House staffer working for the previous administration was a casual friend of an FBI agent who had been copied on an early-on organizational email concerning the investigation of the current President's campaign. In the interval between the agent's being copied on the email and his being reassigned to another matter, then thought more pressing, to wit, the discovery of a computer that may have been used to exchange emails with the former Secretary of Interior's assistant and reputed — by some — lesbian lover, the White House staffer had posted on facebook a picture of himself and the agent at the bachelor party of a common friend. The Congressman's committee had already reviewed the email in the course of its very probing investigation of the FBI when, mysteriously, several days ago the more conspiratorially-oriented sectors of the internet had uncovered and started making much fuss about the facebook post. The Congressman and his crony had responded to this fuss by announcing with great solemnity the existence of the email, the details and recipients of which they made no effort to conceal, and to assure the public and the President that they were taking the entire matter very, very seriously. The former staffer and the agent were both slapped with subpoenas: the Congressman was now promising that, at the hearings, they, the committee, would determine the truth of certain stories that had started circulating the conspiracy sites about overheard conversations between the deponents.

The panelists did not discuss the source of these stories, but dwelled very much upon the fact that Congress would be asking the obvious bad actors about them.

ODOACER

"The truth will come out, Ron. This committee is not going to stand by while the deep state run amok ruins people's lives."

The good news was then announced that the FBI agent had been suspended from duty pending the investigation. And the former staffer had resigned his consulting job.

"Little fucker deserves it," said Ken. "Worse if this is as big as it seems."

BUZZ went the phones, and Ken and Charles quickly read the latest.

Wow! Crooked FBI Agent Keith Eldridge suspended from duty for conspiring with White House against my campaign. Witch hunt! If guilty, consequences will be severe!

Ken slapped the table. "Witch hunt!"

"Damn," said Charles Earl Jarlsberg III, and the two exchanged high fives.

When the program went to commercial, Ken turned to get a better look at his breakfast-mate. "Did you say Charles?"

"Yes."

"Where you from?"

Charles had a backstory. It, along with money and some other necessaries, had been in the envelope Hanno gave him.

"Bucks County Pennsylvania. Outside Philly."

Ken shook his head. "Shit, man. Well, what are you doing out here?"

"I had a friend at the biotech, told me he could get me a job. But it was bullshit."

Ken grimaced. "That's rough, man."

He returned to his breakfast, chewing thoughtfully on a lump of granola.

Then he perked up again. "You thinking of staying out here?"

45

ODOACER

"Yeah," Charles answered. "If I can find work I guess. Good people out here."

Ken smiled. "You got that right. Well, look, if you're staying, I can introduce you to some guys. Good guys." He tapped the red hat that he's tossed into his satchel upon entering the restaurant. "One of them may be able to help you with the job thing."

Charles tensed just slightly. This was it.

He smiled somewhat cautiously at his new friend, and again shook his hand.

"I'd like that," he said. "I'd like that, sure."

It was on.

CHAPTER NINE

A FOOL IN LOVE

The Chevalier Johann Peter Friedrich Ritter von Stilicho had been missing for almost a week. His bed was undisturbed. The minibar was fully stocked. Room service was a thing of distant memory. Mona had grown bored with daytime TV and with trying to engage the maids in smalltalk. They seemed not at all eager to let her practice her Spanish.

On the third day without the Chevalier, Mona had returned to work. After the dizzying escapade at Starbucks, and masquerading as the merry widow Sekshaus, the neat, bright, angular offices — with their tasteful selections of modernish art and sleek pine furniture — seemed almost oppressively uninspired, enervating, even.

Mona read one email after another, so many of them from Sinjenour, who had emailed her almost every hour for a week. Most of these, fortunately, were followed up by apologetic if slightly peeved responses to Mona's out-of-office message, in which the enigmatic master-attorney ordered this or that junior associate, copied, to "pick up the slack" in her absence. Reviewing these, Mona briefly, queasily, with a start entertained the fleeting and possibly, hopefully, illusory notion that she missed the little aristocrat.

ODOACER

Fortunately, before she could proceed too far down this rabbit hole of dread, the broad-shouldered, slightly paunched form of Vin Sinjenour, esquire, appeared in her door.

"Mona!" he exclaimed. "What are you doing here?"

She smiled politely. "The Chevalier has taken on a side project. I couldn't be any use in the hotel, so —"

"A side project?"

"A woman, Vin. The Chevalier met a woman."

Sinjenour cast his piercing eyes floor-ward, just briefly, and made just the hint of a fidget. "Ah yes," he said, haltingly, "I see."

"It's okay. I need to catch up on —"

Sinjenour paced the narrow corridor between the door and Mona's desk. "Yes, the Chevalier, you see, he is a man of taste. Yes. But a man of traditions — perhaps — perhaps hidebound traditions." He rubbed his chin. "He comes from, and represents — perhaps — he exemplifies — a certain — ethos. A way of life if you will. He is the last, I think, and —"

"It's okay, Vin," said Mona, with as much sweetness as she could muster, and, inside, hating herself for, inevitably, feeling it her job to now put him at ease.

"Yes, well," Sinjenour continued. "I hope he hasn't — well. What I mean to say is that we can't hold him to standards that —"

The mighty attorney seemed to shudder then under Mona's stare. Without her even noticing, it had become withering.

"That is not to say — well. Our standards! Yes — our standards. THE LAW!" he proclaimed in capital letters, cupped hand skyward. "Immutable! The immutable LAW."

Mona offered him smile.

"I'm quite able to handle myself, Vin," she said firmly. "And I'm more than capable of handling the Chevalier. I'd better get back to him now." And she thereupon packed up her things — along with a few case files, in case the present idyll with Miriam Roth exceeded her expectations — and left.

48

ODOACER

As luck would have it, the Chevalier returned briefly that evening around eight. He wore white linen pants, rolled up to his knees, a billowing shirt unbuttoned to the navel, and a slightly wilting wildflower tucked behind the ear. "I'm in love," he dreamily proclaimed as he entered, the back of his hand to his forehead. "I'm in love with Miriam Roth!"

But the ebullient mood did not last. When Mona asked him why he was there, the Chevalier confessed — with accelerating panic and despondency — that Miriam had taken the night off to play laser tag with her friends. "Why? Why? Why?" he cried, flinging himself on the bed. "How can she leave me alone like this?" he sobbed. He spun to Mona and asked throatily, "doesn't she know how I ache?"

Mona offered to prepare the Chevalier a cup of tea, or to get him a sandwich, but he instead dissolved into undignified wailing, the moan of which was luckily muffled by the pile of pillows into which he'd burrowed.

Mona had meanwhile found a show on TV — a Japanese medical drama — and tried to ignore the Chevalier. For his part, he eventually came around and started watching himself.

"Who's that?" he asked, tearfully at first.

"I just started watching. The doctor I think."

"Why does she walk that way?"

"I don't know."

"Who's that?" He was calming down.

"Another doctor."

"Is he a bad doctor?"

"I've watched as long as you have, Chevalier. I think he's her rival."

"He's young. Some kind of hotshot."

"Yes, Chevalier. I suppose he'll get his comeuppance."

And later: "I think he's losing the patient. My god."

"Sit tight."

"Oh — Oh, my. Is she allowed to just walk into the operating room like that?"

ODOACER

"It's a TV show."

Still later: "She did it! Mona France, you were right. That young hotshot doctor has learned his lesson."

And so on. By the end, the Chevalier had all but forgotten the name Miriam Roth.

But not quite.

Mona fell asleep during the third episode of the Japanese medical drama. The doctor had again been upstaging a rival in the operating room when she dozed.

When Mona France had awoken, the TV was off and the Chevalier was gone.

It was another five days before he returned. This time Mona had resisted going back to work. When the door opened and the Chevalier strode in, it was a relief.

"Very well," he said, drily, "I have what I need."

"For what?"

"For what I need to do. Mona, we shall return to the museum tomorrow."

And that is exactly what they did.

That day, Mona was not Ottavia Maria Sekshaus, just Mona France. And the Chevalier was not the invalid heir Ferdinand Sekshaus, he was just whoever he was, international jewel thief. They strode into the museum — this time, neither paid the entire recommended donation — avoided the butterfly exhibit, and arrived in the Hall of Gems. It was just after 10:30.

"What happens now?" Mona whispered.

"Just film," said the Chevalier, nonchalantly, "and leave everything to me."

Mona removed her phone from her purse and, as she had been instructed to do, meticulously "documented" each of the aristocrat's moves as he pushed his way to the front of the crowd.

"Is Miriam going to help us?" asked Mona, following in his wake. She felt sick in her stomach. She had never done anything remotely like this.

50

ODOACER

"Not exactly." They were now pressing against the rope. Mona threw up in her mouth and, disgustedly, re-ingested the hot, tingly phlegm-ball.

"She gave you some information, right? You have a plan?"

"Film!"

"Chevalier?"

"After a fashion, my love." With those words, he ducked under the rope, marched up to the case before the guards could react, removed a fine ball-peen hammer from the pocket of his blazer and, with a firm, direct hit, shattered the glass. He then grabbed the sapphire.

"Run, Mona!" he exclaimed as the guards leapt to action and sirens exploded all about them.

Mona was not running. She was hyperventilating.

"Here, you may stop filming now," said the Chevalier, taking the phone gently from her hand. "Come along." Taking her under his arm, he ducked the first guard, then the second, then led the young attorney through the closing gap in the heavy steel doors.

And   then   they   ran.

CHAPTER TEN

OUR NATION'S CAPITAL

The Chevalier had decided that Mona should take the disguise of a tourist. So he had purchased for her a too-large black T-shirt, on which was written, in big hazy letters, "I'm Not As Think as You Stoned I Am," and, below that, in smaller letters, of an entirely different font, "Washington, D.C." She wore this T-shirt and carried a small American flag as she waited at the south end of the South Lawn, waiting for the Chevalier to emerge from his meeting.

She was nervous still, but calm by the standards of the last several days.

After stealing the Cape Town Sapphire, they had calmly, casually left the museum, hailed a cab, and returned to their hotel suites. There, flush with the moment, drugged by the terrifying thrill of felony, by mutual consent, and upon their joint designs, they surrendered to passion.

By this point in the narrative, the reader will have come to expect that the Chevalier was a "generous" lover for whom the principle joy of intercourse lay in giving pleasure to another. This decidedly was not the case. It had been weird,

52

and altogether quicker and less professional than Mona had anticipated, and she already regretted it in the short interval before its end. That afternoon, after a brief nap, she had patiently but firmly told the Chevalier it had been a mistake. He had taken the news with good grace, but there was perhaps something winking in his response that it had been "healthy for our friendship that we got this thing behind us." His subsequent offer to provide a massage was politely refused, magic fingers notwithstanding.

In the days that followed — the Chevalier insisted that they lay low while the police were out in force, per his excellency the mayor's advice — they mostly stayed out of each other's hair, uniting only to see off taciturn Jørgen, with his high-piled wheelbarrow of furniture and cooking supplies, when he set out alone for the Chevalier's much-ballyhooed Alpine hide-out.

Then there was the drive to D.C., excruciating as an emotional matter, but well-timed to avoid traffic, the check-in to the hotel, further avoidance, and finally the planning for the big day — today.

The Chevalier had entered the White House through the service entrance two hours earlier. Mona's loitering by the fence had drawn a few quizzical looks from the secret service, but did not seem to be making any waves.

And then, like that, the Chevalier reappeared.

"Ah, Mona my love. It seems we have made the connection." He took her arm in his — she reluctantly played along — and began strolling south toward the Ellipse.

"What now?" she asked as they neared the Washington Monument. The slightly perturbed Secret Service agents were now far behind them.

"Now I upload everything to the mainframe in my Alpine hide-out." He took out his device, tapped his finger against the screen, and smiled with satisfaction. "It's uploading now," he said, triumphantly, presumably referring to Mona's scrupulous "documentation" of the museum heist as well as whatever evidence he had just collected on his meeting with —

"Did you meet him?"

"Who?"

"The President?"

"Oh, yes!" said the Chevalier. "He's a true gentleman." He glanced at the device. "Still uploading. Once it's transmitted, we shall lay low a couple days, then regroup with taciturn Jørgen at my Alpine hide-out."

"Are you quite sure you need me for that part, Chevalier?"

"Oh yes," he smiled. "That's where it all comes together." He turned to her, suddenly wearing a look of grave concern. "Mona, my dear, I hope that that bit of panting intimacy the other day did not make things — weird — for you."

She grimaced. "I can handle that, Chevalier, but please don't use the term panting intimacy."

"Very well," he said. "Someday, perhaps we can discuss it — in whatever terms you should propose, of course, I hasten to add."

"Let's keep things professional, Chevalier."

"Yes!" He said, "Delightful. Ah? Ah! Ah-hah-hah-hah!" he laughed gaily. "Ah," he exclaimed, just as the gay laugh was tapering gaily off, "it has uploaded." He tapped the screen.

It had happened not a moment too soon. At that moment, a heavy-framed dark gray Lada with tinted windows screeched to a halt beside them.

A smallish man stepped out from the passenger side. He had a weasely face, which he kept mostly in the shadow of a much-dated fedora. His suit was a baggy, ill-fitting gray. His companion, meanwhile — a giant of a man in a too-small gray suit, pastily pale, with a scar on his cheek and long sideburns — stepped out from the driver side, walked around the car, and hemmed in Mona and the Chevalier from behind.

"Comrade Hanno," said the small man, sing-songily, but with a mirthless smile. "Please to come with us."

The Chevalier reddened and waved Mona into the back seat of the Lada. The large man shut the door behind them with a heavy thud.

"It was just a dalliance," said the Chevalier quickly, quietly to Mona while the engine sputtered on. "What do they say? If a man is not at 16? No heart, see?" The Chevalier held quiet for a moment while Mona stared in stupefied amazement.

As the car lurched past the Jefferson Memorial and then along the Potomac, the small man turned to peer at his captives over the top of the front bench.

"Comrade Hanno," he said, "I apologize for this, sincerely."

"For what, old chap?"

The small man raised over the front bench a small dart gun. It fired almost silently: there was just a light poof as the dart left the cylinder, and a lighter still thud as it entered its target. One dart entered Mona France, the other entered the Chevalier. This happened in rapid succession, punctuated only by the slightest flick of the small, ugly man's wrist as he adjusted his aim.

Then the world was black.

CHAPTER ELEVEN

EZIO's NEMESIS

Ken had at length introduced Charles Earl Jarlsberg III to the guys. It wasn't a very stable group — some showed up more often than not, some more often not, and there were cliques within cliques, shifting alliances, and occasional dalliances with outsiders. But in time the group known as the guys took on a certain coherence, if only insofar as a plan to spend the evening drinking with the guys meant an evening drinking with certain guys and not other guys.

Under this working definition, the guys were Ken, Mickey Milliner, an accountant; Mikey Smith, a travel agent; Kasey Farmer, who owned a financial services shop; Crag Miner, vice president of marketing for a soda distributor; Andy Baker, also an accountant; Brian Brewer, who taught economics at the community college; Mike Cartwright, who managed a fitness club; Scott Mason, town clerk; Brian Cooper, a banker; Joey Barber, human resources assistant at the pharma company; Chris Potter, a car salesman; the one they all called Obie, last name unknown, who was always talking about "my business"; the one they called Oise (rhyming with Boise), who never talked about work; Brian Draper, a lawyer at a small local firm; Dan Hunter, who owned a landscaping business; and Jason Tanner, who managed the local affiliate of a Japanese steakhouse chain. And then there was Ezio W. Burgher, who was their unofficial leader. He worked at the plant.

Not one of them understood His Own Interests.

They had a favorite bar, Bernice's, which had linoleum floors, whitewashed concrete walls, and was too brightly lit. It had a juke box over which the guys' various factions had joined issue, some preferring classic rock, some preferring country, while others eagerly proclaimed their appreciation and understanding of rap. Or some rap, anyway. The President's portrait hung over the bar, next to a pair of cherished shot glasses Bernice had acquired in Cabo San Lucas. These were used on the night He won, and had since been retired.

On this evening, Ezio gave Charles a ride. Ezio had helped him get a job at the plant, and since then they had become fast friends taking smokes in the break room and sharing rides to and from work and — lately — everywhere else. Ezio had told him, once, when they were discussing movies, which Ezio loved, that he looked like an actor who, maybe, looks a bit like you.

Bernice didn't have a kitchen, and so she let them bring in outside food as long as they bought a few drinks, which they did. Ezio had brought Chinese for the two of them. He said it was his favorite. Bernice had complained about the smell, but was mollified by the offering of a couple dumplings, which she scarfed down greedily.

They talked about nothing, really. Ezio tried starting a couple conversations about sports, this game or that, but moved on when it became evident that Charles didn't really follow sports.

"Yeah? Not for you?" Ezio had said. He looked handsome with his protruding, somewhat Slavic cheeks, and with the wide triangular planes of his jaws. He was tanned, and his just-graying hair hair arranged in a neat buzzcut. He'd taken off his red had and set it on the table. Charles kept his on.

"I wasn't really into them growing up," he added. "But it's people's lives around here. You learn to love them."

Charles nodded and tried to look comfortable eating chicken fried rice with a fork.

They ended up talking about movies. Ezio liked directors from the 60s and 70s — especially the Italians — both Italian-Americans and Italian-Italians. He went on at great length about Apocalypse Now, both in its original version and in the director's cut, the music, the scenes, and the characters. He held forth on the short but incredibly productive career of the character actor John Cazale and, once suitably drunk, treated Charles to a spotty Marlon Brando impersonation.

It was a good time, a real good time, and gave Charles no cause to think of politics or false consciousness or of any True Interests beyond Ezio's evidently sincere interest in movies. Oh, there was nothing too innovative about his tastes, especially for a man and a man of his age, but he at least showed an appreciation for the art form.

It was a good time until Andrew entered the bar.

"Oh shit, this guy," Ezio muttered. "Fucking Andrew."

Andrew was Ezio's nemesis, a thirty-something glasses-wearing nerd who worked at the bio-tech, didn't come from the town, and wore stylishly ripped jeans. As far as Charles could tell, he and Ezio had crossed paths only once before, but since then Ezio had learned Andrew's name was Andrew and had very recently been developing an entire genre of Andrew jokes. These consisted, in substance, of likening other people's appearances or mannerisms to those Ezio ascribed to Andrew, or imagining how Andrew would react to relatively ordinary situations.

"God, that guy looks like that Andrew guy."

"Kasey's waggin' his hips like he's Andrew or something."

"Can you imagine if that guy Andrew had to operate one of these things?"

"Andrew would probably fall in the lake, you know?"

And so on.

Charles played along, if only to keep up his cover — and because notwithstanding the Andrew jokes he liked Ezio — but he was altogether sure Andrew's antipathy toward Andrew was a projection of false consciousness — a contradiction that would need in time to be recognized and surpassed if Ezio were to understand His True Interests. Just maybe not now.

"He just walked in the bar like he's fucking Andrew or something," Charles whispered as Andrew walked in, getting a little laugh out of his friend.

Andrew's offense had been logged the previous Saturday.

It was a bright, cloudless early afternoon, and the town's wide main street and low-rise store fronts were little shaded by the few straggly saplings that the business development commission had planted a couple years earlier. This exacerbated the ordinary effects of being drunk at 1 in the afternoon. "Damn, that sun's bright," exclaimed Ezio. Charles, who had been drinking with him at Bernice's, instantly wished he'd pissed one more time before leaving Bernice's.

They had managed not to stumble. Ezio's truck was parked two blocks away, at the precise opposite end of the commercial improvement district. But he vowed to get a coffee and rest off his drunk before getting in. They found a bench and sat, Ezio meticulously inventorying every samurai movie he had ever seen.

A traffic light turned green. A black youth — maybe 16 — loped toward them. He slouched a bit, and wore his pants low, too low, on his hips, revealing his boxers down to the pelvis.

The youth had passed them by. And behind them passed the man they would come to know was Andrew. He carried a brown paper bag, probably from the organic grocery that had opened after the biotech.

Ezio flashed him a look. It was a simple, none-to-hostile look of racial solidarity, of a kind most white people can recognize. He simply rolled his eyes, shook his head just slightly, and sighed. After all, the kid's pants were falling down.

Andrew had briefly made eye contact with Ezio, and then looked abruptly away — without an eye roll, without a head shake, and without a sigh — and sped on his way.

A few minutes passed. They watched traffic. Ezio had stopped talking about samurai movies.

"Did you see that fucking prick?" he said at last.

"Who?" asked Charles.

"That fah — That douchebag in the thick glasses. Who the fuck does he think he is?"

"I didn't really notice," Charles lied.

Ezio had slouched on the bench, shook his head. "The prick thinks he's better than me," he muttered.

After that, the Andrew jokes had started.

And now Andrew was in Bernice's. More accurately, Andrew was slumming in Bernice's. Even more accurately, Andrew was slumming in Bernice's with some friends from the biotech.

It was just after ten.

Perhaps they'd finished dinner at one of the new fancy places in town — it was Friday — and wished to continue the revelry at a place they could walk to. Though some grimaced and one or two rolled their eyes, the guys on balance, and Bernice, were willing to give the invaders the benefit of the doubt.

"Sit where you like," said Bernice in the usual indifferent squawk that passed for hardiness.

The visitors pushed together a trio of smaller tables and found spots around it while Andrew, their spokesman, ordered a couple pitchers from the bar.

Ezio nudged Charles' side. He gestured toward Andrew with his eyes and eyebrows, but he didn't seem mad. He was smiling, in fact, like this was too good to be true. "Fucking Andrew — himself — is in the bar," he whispered.

Charles smiled — and couldn't help but to laugh when he made eye contact with Ezio — as Andrew returned to his table with his two pitchers of bad beer.

His look was different from what it had been the other day. He had the same black hair, with longish bangs, but it was combed back in a more professional manner. Instead of a T-shirt he wore a button-up shirt, striped, and instead of jeans he wore slacks.

His friends dressed similarly, with minor exceptions. One, a Sikh, wore a modest turban. Another, black, wore a much more stylish, red velvet shirt and a buzz-cut. And the last was a woman, rather butch, with jowls, hair bunched atop and short on the side, and a button-up denim shirt.

They were talking too loud, laughing, yelling for more drinks.

Ezio was in the spirit.

"Hey," he said to Charles, with the effusion of good nature only excessive beer consumption can engender, "I'm gonna go talk to them."

When Andrew returned to the bar for more pitchers — Bernice had ignored their shouted orders — Ezio smiled. Andrew nodded back and went about his business. Ezio drank more.

When Andrew and his companions played darts, Ezio went over and watched. They never talked to him, except for the woman, named Emily, who smiled politely when Ezio yelped in reaction to a miscast dart. Ezio drank more.

Finally, the night was winding down and Andrew came to the bar to settle. Ezio spun on his stool to address him. "Where are you folks from?"

Andrew seemed surprised Ezio had addressed him, and answered in a cadence that was as much question as answer: "At RevuLife?" he said, referring to the BioTech. "We work together."

"Did You have a good time?"

"Yeah," said Andrew, collecting his change. "Great place."

"Looks like a good crew," Ezio said, nodding toward the assortment of ethnics Andrew had been drinking with.

"Yeah, well." Andrew paused. "Goodnight," he said. And rejoined his friends.

After they'd left, Ezio sat grimly at the bar.

"What's bothering you, Ezio?" asked Charles after it became clear he'd need to ask that question.

"You try to be friendly," said Ezio, shaking his head.

CHAPTER TWELVE

THE CASTLE BY THE SEA

Mona France awoke to find herself in a large, airy, sparsely decorated room. Specifically, she was on a bed in a large, airy, sparsely decorated room, wearing the same awful tourist clothes she'd had on when the Chekists abducted her. Besides that, she had no idea where she was.

There was a heavy oaken door at the far end, on which someone was pounding. Groggy Mona took it as a positive sign that whoever it was was at least pounding.

"Come in," she said.

The door opened a crack and a tall, cadaverous man poked his head in. He wore a neat buzz-cut with sideburns that extended to the earlobes, a bushy goatee, a form-fitting black turtleneck and somewhat baggier camouflage pants. The man said nothing but gestured for Mona to follow him.

"I need a few minutes," she said, as firmly as she could, and the cadaverous man, happily, complied, pulling the door shut behind him.

Mona stepped wobbily out of bed, stretched, and surveyed her surroundings.

ODOACER

The room's far wall was of heavy quarried stone, the other three were plastered and whitewashed. Thick wooden beams held up a slightly dropping ceiling. There was a mirror and a sink, a wardrobe and a bureau — both filled with clothes in what appeared to be her size — and a second, very low door that opened onto a tiny alcove in which Mona found a toilet and a walk-in shower. Ever the renter, she confirmed that the former flushed and the latter was hot.

The decor was minimal: three small, devotional oils evenly spaced along one wall and a gloomy triptych on the bureau. Opposite the troika of devotional paintings was a bank of four deeply-recessed romanesque arched windows through which shafts of bright sunlight entered the cell. Thinking that term apt under the circumstances, Mona checked her phone and found there was no signal and no wifi. Her mailbox had last updated nearly two days earlier with a quartet of plaintiff emails from the great attorney, followed by a quartet of apologies from the same great attorney which also — with unmistakable passive aggression — directed copied junior associates to once again "please fill in for Mona while she's on her trip." She shut the device off.

The view from the windows afforded no hint of where she was, except that she was high above a seacoast. The tops of two wispy pines gave the only indication that there was anything at all between her room and the sea, which, beyond, was a glistening blue overtaken by sheet fog at the horizon.

The knocking resumed. "Five minutes," Mona yelled in response, then stripped, peed, showered, and dressed. The clothing provided had a decidedly antique appeal, but the flapper gown on which she settled nicely complimented her curves. Not that she cared about such things, particularly under the circumstances.

Mona opened the door to find the cadaverous man standing motionless in its frame. Behind him was von Stilicho, checking his watch. "Ah! Mona!" he exclaimed with a wholly delighted smile. She smiled back, grateful that they were at least still in this together, if not sharing the noble jewel thief and failed presidential blackmailer's evident delight.

Von Stilicho had changed into evening wear, also of another era, which he wore with what he would have characterized as dashing élan. "I tried to explain to our shy friend here that a woman needs time," he lamely jested, then added *sotto voce*, "He stared at that door like a dog that entire time."

The cadaverous dog-man must have heard this, but showed no sign of offense. He merely spun on his heel, gesturing for the captives to follow. They did. Through a long arcade and down a stone staircase they tried — but not too hard — to keep up with the strange man's long, loping strides. When they'd fallen sufficiently far behind, Mona stole a glance at her companion and asked, "von Stilicho, do you have any idea where we are?"

The Chevalier twitched, as though surprised Mona would want to know this. "I should say we're in a castle, Mona France," he replied after a moment's thought.

"Yes, von Stilicho, but where is the castle?"

The two were gaining on their escort, who now stood impassively before a set of heavy doors. "I confess I have no idea," whispered von Stilicho at last as they reached the door. "But I suspect some of our questions are about to be answered."

The tall man flung open the doors.

Mona and the Chevalier Ritter von Stilicho stepped out into a sunny garden. Specifically, it was, or it had the appearance of, a medieval herb garden. It was a square, roughly 50 feet on each side, enclosed on two by the mass of the castle and on the other by a mossy stone wall, eight or ten feet high. Neat rows of new growth gave way at the edges to low, bright green bushes with tiny flowers of red, yellow and purple, while reedy grasses clumped before outcroppings of native rock. Birds chirped, bugs buzzed, and, just beyond the wall, the scraggly tops of a half dozen pines stirred gently in the ocean breeze.

ODOACER

Intersecting footpaths divided the garden into quadrants, and at their intersection was a low, round fountain, the water barely trickling from an elevated saucer into the pool below. Along the edge, with back turned to Mona and von Stilicho, sat a figure in a glistening silver muumuu. This figure was feeding sparrows from his outstretched hands, the birds fluttering and chirping about its head and torso in a halo.

The cadaverous dog-man waved the captives in the direction of the muumuued figure and shut the door behind them. Their footsteps crunched along the gravel path. "Our host, it would seem," said von Stilicho softly.

When they were about ten feet away, the figure rose, gently brushed away the sparrows, and turned to his guests.

It was former senior presidential advisor Peter S. Donovan.

"Peter Donovan!" exclaimed Mona.

"Pete!" exclaimed von Stilicho.

It was unmistakably he. His famously splotchy, stubbly skin lay encased in gleaming beige foundation, and in addition to the toe-length silver muumuu he wore a minimalist crystal tiara. But the husky frame, salt-and-pepper pompadour, and snarling lip instantly gave away this most hated presidential confidante.

That was no condemnation. Donovan famously enjoyed being hated. He was, and proudly made himself out to be, a homegrown philosopher and teller of hard truths, usually racist ones. Donovan had built a media empire then chaired the President's campaign before landing a suitably amorphous job on the White House staff. From this perch, he made dark, cryptic pronouncements to grateful press contacts about the President's ambitions and anticipated role in the history of the nation, and he insinuated that he, Donovan, the schemer, had things in mind for this administration that even the President had yet to conceptualize. And yet, within a year, he was out. In playing the heel, Donovan had built little constituency of his own — and when the President saw fit to wipe the slate clean on this or that scandal or string of legislative failures, Donovan had made the most convenient bad-faith counselor, whose officially concealed misdeeds and betrayals could be ritually discovered and expunged. So Donovan was out, or so it seemed.

And now he was holding Mona France — and the Chevalier Johann Peter Friedrich Ritter von Stilicho — captive in what the jewel thief had boldly identified as a castle.

Donovan smiled warmly.

"My guests have awoken!" he exclaimed. "Ritter von Stilicho — do you still go by Hanno?"

"To friends," said the enigmatic nobleman, offering his hand.

"And Ms. Mona France, esquire," the former presidential advisor continued, turning now to the young attorney. She too offered her hand, which Donovan took and — bowing low — kissed. "I am enchanted," he said.

Mona felt, if not, perhaps, at ease, then at least marginally more assured that she wasn't going to have her brains blown out in a basement somewhere.

The former advisor gestured for them to sit with him at the fountain's edge. They did, the Chevalier cupping a handful of water onto his brow.

"I apologize, of course, for the manner in which you were brought here."

"Yes, Pete," interjected von Stilicho, "I was meaning to raise that."

"I'm afraid it couldn't be helped," came the response with a dismissive wave of the hand. "I don't suppose we need to say everything out loud. But, you see, I was worried about you."

"How so, Mr. Donovan?" asked Mona.

The former presidential advisor replied breezily: "I was concerned that, in — ignorance, perhaps — a failure to properly — understand things — you — both of you, would end up interfering in a very, very important project and — I hope not, but — find yourselves in a lot of trouble."

"What project, Mr. Donovan?"

ODOACER

Donovan again rose and began strolling the footpath. Von Stilicho, and then Mona France, followed. "There will be much time to discuss things, Ms. France," Donovan said with a kind, sad smile. "But first, allow me to give you a tour."

He plucked a pair of apples from a gnarled old tree and handed one to each of his guests. The Chevalier dug in.

"This castle, you see, is really quite exquisite," the host — for that is how he would describe himself — told them. He proceeded to tell a long and altogether pointless story about how, with his media fortune, he'd had it brought stone by stone from the Languedoc and reassembled — he paused, catching himself — "here." The castle was named Chateau Trois-Fois-Maître — so-called because of the commanding position it once occupied along an important toll road, busy estuary and — somewhat redundantly — bustling port.

"Yes, I know that one well," said von Stilicho with a wink. "The stories one could tell."

"And no doubt will," jested Donovan before quickly returning to his lecture: "It was built and rebuilt, of course. Burned during the wars of religion, and again during the Revolution." The castle was eventually abandoned, he added somewhat sadly, because it was militarily obsolete and moreover difficult to heat.

"It was the name that got me, of course," the former advisor exclaimed. "For I too am three times the master — of the press, of politics — and," he winked slyly, "of the finer things."

This was a *mot*, a certified *mot*, as Mona would soon come to know. Donovan and the Chevalier lived by them. And when a *mot* is made, one titters, as von Stilicho now tittered at Peter Donovan's *mot*. Mona merely smiled, albeit more politely than mirthfully, causing a flash of disappointment to cross her host's heretofore serene countenance.

"Speaking of the finer things, Pete," spoke up the tittering Chevalier, "is it not, as the saying goes, noon

ODOACER

somewhere." He laughed gaily at this, which was more jest than *mot*, and a rather tired jest at that.

"Yes," replied Donovan. "Yes, how rude of me. Come."

He led his guests to the door.

As he turned his back, von Stilicho tossed the chewed-up core of his apple in a low arc over the wall. It was instantly vaporized in an electric forcefield.

Donovan turned to his guests and with the usual (it seemed) bored serenity said: "A necessary safety precaution, I'm afraid. The cliff is nearly four hundred feet — and even if one survives the fall, the sea is infested with sharks. Now, come."

They came.

The tour was excruciating. When Donovan wasn't recounting his heroic days as an up-and-coming media investor, he was describing the castle and its contents in terrifyingly boring detail. In its current incarnation, the interior was done up in Dutch Renaissance style, a rather strained fit for the thick-walled medieval fortification, that anticipated Graceland by 300 years. Most of the rooms — a smoking room, a map room, a billiards room, a parlour, a study, et cetera — were slathered in gaudy greens and reds, detailed in gold, and overdecorated with candelabra, scientific contraptions, and the assembled portraiture of generations of absurd local potentates. The exceptions were along the west side, where the captives' rooms were, along with a sleek, bright, angular dining room, its westernmost wall a single great sheet of glass overlooking the ocean fog below.

Here, a second tall, cadaverous, dog-man — much like the first but for reddish flecks in his goatee — served wine on a silver tray.

"Ah," exclaimed Donovan with a sly grin to his guests. "At last! The refreshments I promised." He fixed a penetrating glance at the dog-man, who jolted into action, serving Mona, von Stilicho, and at last the Lord of Trois-Fois-Maître before resuming his post by the door.

"To *my* master," Donovan said, holding his glass aloft, "Lord Bacchus!"

This time Mona had the wherewithal to titter.

The Chevalier sipped, sighed, and nodded gratefully to his host. After he had, he placed an elegant, perfectly-manicured hand on the sleeve of Donovan's majestic muumuu and said, "Pete, I could not help but notice how efficient your household staff is, but they haven't so very much to say."

In response, Donovan offered his serene, knowing, concealing smile and led his guests out of the dining hall and into a grim, soot-stained corridor lit by candelabras.

"My Proud-boys are — loyal," he said, "but I'm afraid they don't provide much company."

"Do they ever talk?" Mona asked.

He shook his head sadly. "It is better that they don't. It is safer — and happier — for them — that their lives be — compartmentalized." His manner of pausing every second or third word suggested that his entire summary was a string of carefully-chosen euphemism, but circumstances were still too murky for the presumptively sinister intent to come across. "They are in any event well compensated," Donovan added.

"Compensated how?" Mona prodded.

"Why — in pride of course." The Lord of Trois-Fois Maître had led them to a high, recessed door flanked by marble cherubs.

"Pride? Pride in what?"

Donovan again smiled, although this time there was an unmistakable hint of malice under the serenity. He winked and flung open the door.

"My trophy room!"

The trophy room was a cozy affair, nearly as high as it was wide, with an enormous arched stone fireplace — lit and roaring — flanked by recessed nooks that were lined with bookshelves. In each nook was a high stained glass window. The furniture consisted of a throne and an over-stuffed love-seat facing the hearth, and an end table on which rested an overwrought silver sculpture. The trophies, such as they were,

were the mounted heads of various farm animals: pigs, sheep, many cows — milk cows — and improbably a chicken. Donovan took the throne and his guests shared the love seat, Mona fitting as much of herself into as little space as possible to avoid unnecessary — and, she was sure, half-intentional — brushes with the jewel thief.

"Pete, I must confess I am impressed by your collection," said von Stilicho, gesturing toward the lifelessly-staring head of a Holstein.

The host threw his head back with what seemed like immense satisfaction and happily exhaled. "Yes," he responded. "It is a weakness, I suppose. But a man must test himself."

"Hear hear!" said the Chevalier, offering his nearly-empty glass for a second toast.

A moment later, a third Proud-boy had entered with another tray of wine glasses and, this time, a box of cigars. Mona politely refused the cigar.

"I hunt, of course," muttered von Stilicho, igniting his Monte Cristo. "An avid hunter. Yes, and more. I should be glad to hear of any discoveries you have made in the field of natural science."

Mona grimaced, remembering the dog in Central Park.

"I'm afraid I'm just a simple sportsman."

"Ah!" coughed von Stilicho. "Sport, science — both are merely forms of mastery, are they not?"

"I suppose so," answered the Lord of Trois-Fois-Maître, "and there is so much one must master." As though controlled by the former presidential advisor's stare, an ambling Proud-boy crossed the room and offered him a light. Peter S. Donovan exhaled a mouthful of smoke and stared at the fire.

Mona France broke the silence.

"Mr. Donovan, why have you taken us here?"

Donovan smiled, tight-lipped, and after a long pause spoke: "The devil knows his own, Ms. France." This was said darkly — without the breezy almost new-age wonderment that had heretofore marked Donovan's cadences, and that so nicely matched the muumuu. Mona felt the chill.

"Meaning?"

"Meaning, you and your friend here amassed certain — information — certain compromising information — on a very important man — and I couldn't take the chance you would — well. So I had my friends pick you up and bring you here."

"Suppose we did," Mona said, "acquire information as you say. Wouldn't the public have a right to know it?"

Donovan puffed on his cigar as though lost in thought. "First, Ms. France, and I suspect you know this, the public won't care. Your information will merely confirm what they already knew, for better and for worse. To the nation" — he used this word with a certain strange emphasis — "it will merely confirm this — man — is a hero, fighting for them. To the rest," he gestured contemptuously to the fire, "well, I suppose they'll have one more reason to hate him, to hate us. But they'll also have one more reason to know that they can never, ever defeat us."

Mona frowned. "And second?"

"Second," Donovan smiled, "and I'm sure you know this, you have no intention of going to the public. You want leverage, Ms. France, you want someone to know that you know that he knows that you know. And from that you hope to obtain some minor advantage. To influence policy I suppose. To control, in some small, annoying way a great man. Am I wrong, Ms. France?"

Mona sipped her wine — all of it — and looked to the Chevalier, who, to her immense irritation, had busied himself inspecting a snow globe he'd taken off the mantlepiece.

"And what's wrong with influence, Mr. Donovan?" she replied at last.

The Lord of Trois-Foir-Maître stood up and dreamily inspected the other knickknacks along the mantlepiece. He found a small metal statue of a drunken frog — evidently purchased at a Mexican tourist destination — and lovingly polished it with the sleeve of his muumuu.

He thereupon sighed. "The President has more important things to do than answer to your mundane whims, Ms. France. He has a mission, a world-historic mission, to accomplish. And he must be — focused."

"And what is that mission, Mr. Donovan?"

"Why, don't you know, Ms. France? Have you seen the — hats?" Donovan chuckled.

Mona of course remembered the red hats. Could it really be so stupid? She recited the slogan: "to Make America G—"

Donovan smiled warmly and raised his hand. "Stop there," he said softly. "That is all we mean to do, Mona France. That's it. The greatness will come in time."

As if on cue, two immense Proud-boys came to the former presidential advisor's side. As they did, a piece of wood paneling in the wall slid open to reveal a dark, cobblestoned corridor lit by dim blue lights. "And now, I must take my rest," said Donovan.

"One more thing, Pete," said von Stilicho, rising to his full unimpressive height and still puffing away on his cigar.

"Yes?"

"Are we free to leave?"

Donovan chuckled mirthlessly at this. "That is a philosophical question. One I cannot answer."

The Chevalier rephrased it. "May we go?"

"No, Ritter von Stilicho, you may not," Donovan replied, and with his flanking Proud-boys disappeared into the corridor. The panel slid firmly shut behind them.

The Chevalier looked to Mona and grimaced with what seemed, at most, a kind of light embarrassment over someone else's bad manners.

Mona couldn't help but notice that the host had not called him Hanno.

CHAPTER THIRTEEN

PRISONER OF CONSCIENCE

It was not afraid. It was never afraid. It could not be afraid because it was not weak. It was the opposite of weak.

It was the holy *ka* and *it* saw all unblinkingly. *It* contemplated all and gave thanks. All was light. All that passed passed according to a plan that it called *the* plan. It did not know how things would end, out there, but as time was outside of it, it was outside of time. It had reached its end, which had never been an end but a union with the infinite. Whatever happened out there was — nothing. It saw all this unblinkingly and prayed.

Yet! It couldn't help watching. There was something instructive in a tale playing out in time — in *this* tale — something enthralling. It wanted to see. It had a sense, a very real and profound sense, that in this tale it was in some very important way — *the hero!*

The universe resolved itself into a conventional view. Flare-ejecting binary star systems, floating equations, almond-eyed bodhisattva and more rearranged themselves into the ordinary: a desk, windows, a carpet. The thing a man sees when he wakes up in the morning.

The drapes were drawn, but the dull, gray early morning light peeked in, cutting a sliver across the floor and the bed. The man was in bed.

The room was large, airy, with old, solid — expensive — but not familiarly luxuriant furniture. Yesterday's clothes lay in piles on the floor and tossed, inside-out, over the backs of chairs. The staff had been told in precise terms not to rouse the room's occupant, or to enter the room, or to straighten up, unless expressly directed to do so. With much shouting and many promises of firings, a compromise had been reached. The room would not be locked, but would not be entered, either, except by permission.

A phone lay on the bed stand. Next to it, a clock showed the time: 5:40 a.m.

Manically, a hand jutted out. It took hold of a sleek rectangular iPhone that had been charging on the lower shelf of the bed stand, right next to the Cape Town Sapphire. The latter had ceased to be of any interest. But the phone was always alluring. A pudgy finger of extremely ordinary length tapped in a passcode. The screen came to life. The Twitter application opened.

It watched this with saintly indifference. But it watched.

The finger scrolled up and down the screen, pausing here and there on a pungent or clever reply. Up, then down. Then to the top, to the last published messages.

It hardly read the posts — just took a peek — just to prove it had transcended the need to do so — but it sensed the burning hot rush of *Them*, stirring Themselves to a familiar fury. The body was lifting, the feet hitting the floor. It read.

> Fake News media (disgraceful!) as usual has it wrong. No one tougher on Russia than me. Even crooked critics and haters agree . . .

ODOACER

And so forth. The tweets continued in this fashion over two or three recent posts.

"Russia could bully FIFA, and the world, under weak American leadership. Not anymore! . . ."

"It's soccer, by the way. Sorry, Russia. Football's a much tougher sport . . ."

The hand slammed the device angrily onto the bed stand and reached for the landline.

A cheerful female voice greeted the ear: "Good morning, Sir. How may we help you today?"

The voice that responded came out in a hoarse growl. "Freundhein," the voice said. "Get me Freundhein."

"Yes Mr. Pres—"

The hand slammed the receiver back into its cradle.

The body lifted. It could sense Them exulting in the effort but paid little mind.

Across the room, paused before a mirror, the President's image glared back at it. Always glaring these days. But it understood. *They* were under tremendous pressure and the glare had its effect. It carried a certain old-world authority — not of a king, perhaps, but of a drill sergeant, or an especially stern grocer, suspiciously eyeing his customers. It was for little people a relatable kind of authority. There was no denying that. Mouth clenched, eyes screwed up, forehead slightly tensed. Otherwise, it was the same old face: older, wrinklier, jowlier, perhaps oranger than it had once been, and with wily sprouts of hair shooting off in all different directions pre-preening. But, it decided, the face was not unhandsome. Yes, in that it had been lucky.

The body lumbered to the adjacent bathroom and, opening the spigot in the sink, splashed some water in the face. It felt Them stir, perk up. Unlike Them — They were excitable — it was never any more or less awake; that's how it was when one experienced all of being in a single unblinking glimpse. The sensations They emanated were only of passing, academic interest.

The bedside phone rang and was picked up.

ODOACER

"Yes?"

"Mr. President. It's Freundhein."

"Freundhein," came the reply. "Freundhein." The voice was fuming. "I don't get this."

"Get what, sir?"

"This shit. Tell them I don't get this."

There was a pause before Freundhein replied, rather meekly, "Yes, I understand. I will try to communicate that to my contact."

"I think you'd better, Freundhein."

"Yes, sir, Mr. President."

The President was breathing heavily, almost hyperventilating into the phone. Freundhein stammered, making a hesitant "errrrrr."

"What, Freundhein?"

"Well, sir," he said. "I'll talk to my contact, like I said. I can't guarantee anything, of course. But, sir? Don't you think maybe they would have gamed this all out?"

The President sighed. It could not tell what was going on. It sensed nothing from the high spirits that had been howling moments ago. There was no sensation at all. The doctor was right, of course. The doctor was always right.

Look, Freundhein," the President said at last, cajolingly. "Just tell them, first of all, as always, thanks. And, second, that's just not — me. Tell them just to — you know, tone it down."

"Yes, Mr. President. Of course Mr. President."

"Thanks, Freundhein," the President replied politely. Then, after Freundhein's line went dead, the rush of heat and agitation swarmed back, enveloping it, and the receiver was slammed back down in its cradle so hard that it cracked.

From there, the day proceeded drearily, and, bored, it hung back, paying little thought to the flutter of meetings, briefings and reviews to which the horrid chief of staff subjected the poor man. They were indifferent too, or at least they hardly stirred, except once or twice when the staff chief's hectoring and silent judgment became really, truly too much to bear. There'd be a burning or fluttering sensation here or there and the man would speak: a decision would be made, and the day could at last go on in peace.

So it went until the afternoon. That was when it had — and it wouldn't have thought this possible, being outside of time and what not — its little revelation.

The man had been invited to an event commemorating the life and works of the author Herman Melville. The occasion and venue are not so important. The man was taken to a small library lined with original editions of the author's works, as well as books that were, or would have been, in his library — ubiquitous works like bibles and commentaries, nautical reference works, old magazines and the like. On the wall were pictures — of the author, of his family, of the sea, of whales — and maps, nautical maps, New York maps, Nantucket maps, etc. The man had been seated in an overstuffed armchair next to another, just like it, in which the museum's curator sat: a balding, spindly little man with an American flag pin appended to the lapel of his cheap suit. The event had been billed as a celebration of American literature, and, to a lesser degree, of America's contribution to world literature, and of a uniquely American voice capturing a uniquely American being. That was why the man — at his aides' suggestion, and with Freundhein's hearty approval — was attending.

The man had refused the walking tour of the museum. The man hardly exchanged any private remarks with the curator. They had merely assumed their seats and waited a few moments while the cameras and their operators filed in. Then introductions were made and the man made his remarks.

These went according to form. As the curator nodded along half-idiotically, and the other half idiotically, too, the man spit out a set of random observations on Melville's life and works. The man said Melville's name like it was being said for the first time, as though introducing the most recently-discovered genius — the man used that word, "Genius — A great — Genius" — to the world. Then the man said a few things about the author's life — all the things that, he said, most people didn't know, or hadn't heard about, and that most people would be surprised to find out — and about where, rankings-wise Melville fell in the pantheon of American writers. Then a few cursory remarks about this particular museum and the work it was doing, and name checks for the curator and various staff members and scholars whose names had been written phonetically on little note cards the man held both-handed and hunched over, but that were still mispronounced.

As all this swirled about, it did its usual thing. It meditated and prayed. It gave thanks, and it trusted in the plan, which, in any case, was already accomplished fact, because it was already communing at the level of the infinite and eternal and wasn't exactly here any more than it was any- and everywhere the man had ever been or would ever be, at every moment the man had ever lived through or would live through, and beyond.

But it couldn't help noticing.

On the man's lap was a book, Moby-Dick, opened. The man wasn't reading it, They weren't reading it, but the words were there in front of it. As the man said something about "lots of people" who were coming around to appreciate the works of Herman Melville, it read:

"For, at such times, crazy Ahab, the scheming, unappealingly steadfast hunter of the white whale; this Ahab that had gone to the hammock, was not the agent that so caused him to burst from it in horror again. The latter was the eternal, living principle or soul in him; and in sleep, being for the time dissociated from the characterizing mind, which at other times employed it for its outer vehicle or agent, it spontaneously sought escape from the scorching contiguity of the frantic thing, of which, for the time, it was no longer an integral."

Later, as the event wound up, as the press reluctantly dispersed after having their latest questions ignored, as the curator and his staff were bid a disinterested and distracted

ODOACER

adieu, as the black-eyed secret service escorted the man out, it had a thought. It was a very weird thought, because it was very — very — pinned to the now. It shook when it had this thought. It wasn't supposed to have this thought. And the thought was:

"What about me?"

CHAPTER FOURTEEN

LORD BACCHUS IN THE HEARTLAND

Ezio and Charles arranged to meet the guys at Bernice's for a few rounds. The official occasion was Charles' birthday.

Only about five other guys were there when they arrived. Not Ken, who'd been out of town lately on what he said was business. But Kasey, Crag, Joey, Chris and Obie had all found their way in by seven, and Mikey would arrive a little later. Conversation was stilted and desultory at first. Ezio would have preferred to talk to just Charles, and Joey and Chris were intent on discussing a game no one else had watched. Kasey was sad about something and Crag and Obie barely looked up from their phones.

The drinkers were quickly drunk, and most of them were drinkers, and so the usual debates ensued regarding country, classic rock and rap, this team or that one, Andrew jokes, and town gossip, especially firings, deaths and impregnations.

"Did you hear Carl Jespersen died?"

"Who?"

"Carl Jespersen. In the big white house on Maple."

Pause.

"Used to own the Dairy Cream."

"Oh. That old bastard. He was still alive?"

"Was."

"Wasn't he related to Jenny Fugliero?"

"His wife's niece."

"She was a nice piece of ass."

"Still is. Heard she just got knocked up."

"No shit. Who?"

"Bill FitzHugh."

"Shit. Didn't he just get canned at the A&P?"

"Yep."

And so on.

And so it proceeded, another night at Bernice's, too brightly lit, too little decorated. At one point, sometime around 8:30, Brian C. — who'd arrived late and in boisterous spirits — and Joey tried leading the gang in a rendition of Happy Birthday, but they all trailed off around the second "to you," fated never to revive it.

As more beer poured, the mood eased, and before long they were in something like a group discussion about — it didn't really matter — fishing or something. They were talking for the sake of talking, and no one was overly invested in the subject matter.

And then at nine Bernice turned up the TV.

The occasion was the start of a favorite commentary program, this week being hosted by a slightly less manly version of the usual man behind the desk. Specifically, the substitute was younger, scrawnier, and not quite as abusive as the beloved regular, and thus posed him no threat in his absence. The guys watched with minimal interest for the first 15 minutes, reviving their discussion of fishing during the breaks and occasionally at the substitute host's expense until, inevitably, Bernice shushed them. But then came the Mexicans segment.

It was more a Hondurans or even an El Salvadorans segment, but the distinction, a fine one, was largely missed.

ODOACER

"After the break," the substitute host had teased before the break, "immigrant convoy heading toward the border, and the President says no way. Stay tuned."

That had raised a few heads. A rush of drink orders momentarily swamped Bernice while the guys prepared for some fun.

"I saw something about this," offered Joe. "They have no respect whatsoever for our laws."

"Of course not," replied Obie, "a boilermaker, Bern. Thanks. They don't."

"First thing you do when you enter a country is break the law —" Chris had heard this somewhere, and was repeating it authoritatively now — "you don't belong here."

"My neighbor's Mexican," Kasey volunteered. "Okay guy."

"I'm sure he is," Joe answered. "This is about the law, you know?"

"Well, yeah, the law, and the law says they shouldn't be here," was Chris' response.

Ezio kept quiet.

With the exceptions of him and Charles, the guys were suitably amped up when the segment finally started.

The occasion was that a bus full of fifty Central Americans, who all said they were fleeing gang and domestic violence, was officially (allowing for reasonable traffic) within a day's drive of Tijuana. Their plan was to apply for asylum upon reaching the border. They would thereupon become asylum seekers and would be admitted to the country legally while their applications were pending. But the distinction was another one of those fine ones.

"Goddamn illegals," muttered Chris — clearly he was the hardened thinker of the group — shaking his head.

"Like I said," Joe said, softly, not wanting to upset Bernice, "we've got to be able enforce the laws or this country will be —"

"Overrun," volunteered Obie.

83

ODOACER

"That's what the President is trying to do," proclaimed Kasey with a sudden, nervous passion.

"Shh," went Bernice. They were talking over the show.

BUZZZ.

Devices were checked.

"We must secure our border against illegal crossings," the President had written. "#Stop the Convoy."

"Hell yeah!" cried Kasey.

"He's right," said Joe. "It's about—"

BUZZZ.

As Executive, it is my job to enforce the LAWS in this country, including those on our sacred border. ICE working very hard, but we need more resources.

"Exactly," Joe concurred.

A guest on the show — a sixty-something newspaper columnist with bushy eyebrows — was speaking. As their phones fell silent, the guys watched. He was saying, ". . . is it cruel? Well, one, it's not cruel. We're enforcing the law."

"That's right," said Chris.

"Fuck, I don't care if it's cruel," said Joe, "it's got to be done. It's the fucking law. The other clowns had, what, eight years? to change it if they wanted to."

BUZZZ.

The President: "When I enforce laws, handed to me by my opponents, by the way, I am attacked by the crooked media for being 'cruel.' No, law enforcement. Very dishonest!"

All of the guys, Ezio included, stared at Joe in astonishment.

"Damn," said Kasey.

Joe beamed with pride.

The bushy-browed man continued: ". . . and it's important to understand that, despite what the media tells you, the laws the President is enforcing were enacted by a Congress in which the other party had the majority . . ."

Bernice's erupted in cheers. A toast was made, to Joe, the prognosticator, to the bushy-browed man, to the President. Even Ezio sidled up, in his quiet way, and raised a class. "God damn." He spoke quietly, his voice almost a whistle. Charles Earl Jarlsberg III hoisted his mug as well, struck nearly dumb by such pervasive and complete blindness to everyone's True Interests.

"To ICE!" he proclaimed at last, not knowing what else to say.

"To ICE!" went the guys.

BUZZZ.

The President: "ICE agents are the great, unsung heroes of our fight to protect our borders. Americans of all races and ethnicities should be toasting ICE."

Cheers, again.

Charles Earl Jarlsberg III blanched. He excused himself, hastily, and headed for the door. He had to throw up.

As he stepped out into the chilly night air and emptied his lunch onto the parking lot, Charles Earl Jarlsberg III, that least metaphorical of men, noted with a literal shiver that the coyotes — from different hilltops and different directions, each pack answering and one-upping the shrieks of the last — were all howling at the full moon.

CHAPTER FIFTEEN

CENA DONOVANOSIS

Days and then weeks passed languidly in Chateau Trois-Fois-Maître. Life had taken on a stifling but not altogether disagreeable routine. Each day, Mona took breakfast in her room. Each day, with rare exceptions, the three of them — she, von Stilicho, and former presidential advisor Peter S. Donovan — ate lunch and dinner (or dinner and supper in von Stilicho's parlance) in the dining hall, then later repaired to the trophy room for cigars, aperitifs, and discussion. In the intervening hours, Mona found time to exercise in an old gym, to catch the news on the one TV she could find — an old vacuum-tube affair situated in a cabined in the billiards room — and to think in the herb garden. Out of sheer boredom, she was on-again-off-again banging the Chevalier, who spoke of the whole thing as a grand seduction, but it was never very satisfying and, due to its inevitable brevity, largely failed even as a means of passing time.

The weather had been consistently pleasant — never very hot, seldom cold — long periods of sun alternating with fogs, particularly in the evenings and early mornings. This, along with the sun's dutiful settings over the sea, convinced

Mona and von Stilicho that they were on the West Coast, possibly in California.

This supposition tended to find confirmation in Donovan's interminable mealtime monologues. The master of, *inter alia*, the finer things, invariably went on at tedious length about the offerings — provenance, microclimates, techniques of horticulture, husbandry, and harvesting, as the occasion warranted, regional varieties, genetic engineering, new-fangled and old, et cetera. While he was, or seemed, careful to avoid identifying specifically where anything came from, the items he described as fresh and local — items like wine and fruit and fish — tended to come from that part of the world.

Beside the descriptions of food and drink, which were atmospheric but pointless, the conversation embraced the arcane and esoteric. Mona ignored as much of these as she could, though she couldn't shake the suspicion — in the rare moments that she paid attention — that both men were performing for her, as though they'd convinced themselves and each other that they were warring for an impressionable younger mind from, say, the standpoints of romanticism and enlightenment. Which was a strange thing to think given the content of the meandering, frequently heated conversations, that — far from plumbing the metaphysics of morals or the epistemological premises of great political systems — included, in no particular order: the Civil War and Civil War reenactment (both confessed themselves avid re-enactors); the Police Academy movies; the works of Karl May (which both proclaimed "life-altering"); a historical novel Donovan was working on about Queen Fredegund, which he said had "erotic elements" but, contra von Stilicho's repeated urgings, was "not erotic"; ports, always ports; and wine, wine, wine.

The last topic brought out the absolute worst in both men, each of whom would hold forth long after the other had stopped listening — and long, long, long after Mona has stopped pretending to listen — on the unassailable objective basis for his preferences.

"California, well," would say the Chevalier, tauntingly. "But we know, don't we, that the French do it so much better. And why shouldn't they? Two thousand years of practice — that makes a difference."

"So by that measure," Donovan would shoot back, "the Greeks should have everyone beat."

At which point they'd both make disgusted faces and titter gently at what passed for a *mot* these days.

And so on.

Mona and von Stilicho had also managed to scout out as much of the castle as was open to them. They concluded at length that Trois-Fois-Maître occupied the tip of a peninsula or island, that the electric forcefield ran as much of its perimeter as they had been able to probe, and that there was a garage somewhere in the building from which vehicles came and went with some frequency. They were also able to identify at least twelve distinct Proud-boys.

"Of course, there's likely more than that," the Chevalier had said.

"Okay, fine, von Stilicho, could you try a bit lower please."

"Yes, I think I'm finished, actually" the jewel thief had replied, promptly rolling over and falling to sleep with a muttered, insincere, "sorry."

Such were the languid rhythms of Chateau Trois-Fois-Maître.

What bothered Mona France — apart from the fact they were being held captive and how comfortable the routine had become — was that she still did not understand, really, what Donovan was up to. Oh, sure, he was somehow controlling the President of the United States, probably through some subtle means of blackmail — he'd all but admitted that. But he'd spoken of a project, and more — of a nation and making America — full stop. He'd suggested, also not subtly, that if their blackmail interfered with his blackmail, this could go off the rails. Which of course it had, and which of course was why they were here. But surely Peter Donovan wasn't all hot air — was he?

Mona made it her purpose to find out.

The dinner on May __ began and ended like any other, with the Proud-boys hauling out one course after another and Donovan, in excruciating detail, explaining the history, preparation, and above all the cost of the provisions. Afterwards they repaired to the trophy room for aperitifs, and there the discussion took on a new, more charged air.

But that would come a bit later. First, von Stilicho had to say his piece. In this instance it was — again, seemingly, though Mona had lost track of his ramblings — a meditation either on his youth or on his family's history. It wasn't clear which. It was emphasized, again, that his family — specifically, "the direct line, at least" — were at all relevant times avid consumers of Allied radio — when circumstances permitted — and would gladly look the other way should the R.A.F. make the occasional airdrop onto their estates. Against this backdrop, von Stilicho described in rather too much detail a love affair with one Mette, "an inappropriate woman," said he, who came from the local *haute bourgeois*. She was the youngest daughter of the hated Lottrup clan, to be exact, and yet — von Stilicho spoke movingly, with what was real and surprising affection — things unsaid and avoided giving the plain impression that the girl had died.

He put out his cigar in a small porcelain ashtray, lowered his brow for a moment and then added, with incongruous levity, "ah, but here I am, blubbering like a typical American sentimentalist. It is time for me to get home, Pete."

The Lord of Trois-Fois-Maître smiled and ignored the implicit request.

"And what of you, Ms. France?"

"What?" asked Mona testily, well into her third quaff.

"Where are your people from?"

Mona paused for a moment, thought. For all the Chevalier's talk of American sentimentalism — and this assuredly was not the first time he'd lit on that trope — she had mythologized her life and her origins a good deal less than the celebrated nobleman-cum-jewel-thief. She supposed her grandparents, who she'd at least known, came from somewhere, and there were stories of this or that ancestor having served in this or that conflict — but beyond that —

"I'm not completely sure," she said at length. "Scots Irish, I think, mostly. Some Irish-Irish. And some German. What do you call it? Palatine? Yes. Beyond that? I don't know. White trash I guess."

Peter Donovan flinched. The former presidential advisor briefly removed his crystal tiara. He kneaded his brow forcefully betwixt thick fingers until splotches of foundation had been wiped off.

He smiled sadly at the attorney.

"Is that all you think of them?" he asked. His tone was one of concern — but something of challenge, even malevolence, crept in.

Mona smiled back and sipped her wine.

"I love my family, Mr. Donovan. But whatever their stories are — were — It's not an —"

She fumbled for the right word. What she meant to say, what she felt, was that it wasn't a single story, with a through-line — that her present existence and circumstances bore no teleological relation to the struggles of generations of hapless persons she'd never, ever know, but who were directly related to her. But she wasn't sure how to say —

"It's not what, Ms. France?" Donovan prodded her.

She sat abruptly erect in the love-seat. "It's not an epic, Mr. Donovan."

The former presidential advisor, whose gaze had been forlorn, looked up and met her eye. He smiled, broadly and sincerely, and looked as though he was almost on the point of tears. When he spoke again, his airy, evangelical serenity returned in force:

"Why, Ms. France," he exclaimed, "of course it is. Of course it is an epic. And the climax is now, Ms. France" — he lightly clapped one clenched fist into the other cupped palm —

ODOACER

"Now. In our lifetimes. We are making it happen, you see." Donovan had the nearest Proud-boy refill everyone's glass and greedily downed the contents of his.

"I had been hoping to avoid politics, Pete," interjected the Chevalier, gloomily.

"Nonsense, Hanno," Donovan snapped. "You don't mind Ms. France?"

"Please continue."

"In our lifetimes, Ms. France," he continued. "This President is making it happen. We are making it happen,"

"What are you making happen, Mr. Donovan?" she asked.

"We are forging a nation, Ms. France. A real nation. Out of your 'white trash' and lots of other 'white trash' besides. We are forging a real, honest-to-god nation."

Mona frowned. "We have a nation, Mr. Donovan."

"Not really," he shot back. "Not the way I understand the term. Not presently."

Mona sipped her drink. She could have asked: how do you understand the term, Mr. Donovan? But Mr. Donovan's views were well known. And Mona France was not about to enact — to draft, even — the catechism of Saint Peter. He understood nation to mean people, *a* people, bound by — not laws, not borders, not even customs — but by an attitude — or maybe not even that. United by the direction in which they were all running, and who they were running behind — and defined with reference and in antithesis to all those not running or all running elsewhere. Mona wanted no part of it.

"Thank you, Mr. Donovan," she said, as politely as she could. "I am not interested in being part of your epic or your nation."

"Oh, you're already part of it," the former advisor spoke airily, waved dismissively.

"No, I am not, Mr. Donovan."

Donovan slouched a bit in his throne. "You're just a snob is all." He said this with a taunting, self-satisfied smile —

91

ODOACER

like he wanted to say something — just, mean — and had now said it.

"Excuse me?"

He smiled bitterly. "Oh, I know we have to work on — aesthetics. I mean, yes, I understand why you said 'white trash.' I understand the contempt and the — the fashionable aspects of all this. We need to work on — some things."

"What are you talking about, Mr. Donovan?"

"Yes, Pete," the Chevalier chimed in. "Please explain."

"We need people like you, Mona. You belong too. And I know — I know — the — red hats and crying eagles — I don't do the graphics on Hammer News, but they're — effective. But not really appealing, I see that."

"Mr. Donovan, this is not about aesthetics."

Donovan smiled meekly. "Come now, it is. I mean, it is at least a little. There is a — a sentimental connection we are not — not yet — conveying to you — not convincingly."

"I have beliefs —"

"Sure, sure," Donovan cut her off. "I'm sure we can work on those. But I want — well, here, try this. Think maybe of Norman Rockwell or — no — Grant Wood. You're familiar, yes? Big murals!" He held his hands as wide apart as they would go. "Stevedores with no shirts on. Or firemen with no shirts on shoveling coal, maybe — farmers with no shirts on — big beams lifted by cranes — digging wells — overalls and stuff, do you see what I mean?"

She didn't.

"Okay, okay," said the manic former advisor. "Beatniks. Jack Kerouac. A bunch of guys — poor guys — in the back of a pick-up truck. And they stop for the night and — beans over the fire and — a can of 'em — someone sings! And it's —" he gestured about as though conducting music — "soulful. And — see?"

Mona folded her arms across her chest and shared a short, severe look with von Stilicho, who'd by now fallen completely, bitterly silent.

ODOACER

"Mr. Donovan," she said schoolmarmishly, "ours is a nation of laws."

Donovan cackled bitterly.

"You don't believe that?" she pressed.

"That's not what a nation is. A nation *has* laws."

"We have laws."

"But a nation isn't defined by law."

"Sure it is, it can be," Mona protested.

"What law, Ms. France?"

"The Constitution for one."

"An instrumentality."

"A what?"

"You're the lawyer, Ms. France. That's how the courts once described it, Ms. France. An instrumentality — a tool for the people."

"That's fine —" Mona's voice had become sharper, and louder too.

"*Not* a means of defining the people."

"Meaning what?"

"Meaning —" the Lord of Trois-Fois-Maître rose, stoked the fire, and turned once more to his guests. "Meaning —" he said bitterly — "have you ever seen anything more ridiculous than a Pakistani hanging an American flag from his front porch? I mean, honestly?"

Save the crackle of the fire, silence fell over the room.

Mona France could have said many things, but there was nothing to say. The mask was off Peter S. Donovan, former senior advisor to the President of the United States. The airy charm, the new age sensibilities, the tedious epicureanism dissolved into a simple, bitter taunt that, as much as anything, was the man himself and his movement too. He had offered up image after image — stevedores, firemen, farmers, beatniks, soulful hobos, most of them shirtless — in the expectation that they would stumble upon an America they could share. And when Donovan finally found an image that — well — it was only to express contempt — it was to his mind the *reducto ad absurdam* of a counterfeit America.

93

ODOACER

Mona frowned. "I think we have nothing more to discuss tonight, Mr. Donovan. Thank you for the wine."

Donovan shook his head bitterly as two Proud-boys came to his sides.

"Yes, Ms. France, goodnight. Goodnight, von Stilicho." The panel opened and Donovan entered the tunnel with his escort.

Once again, the panel shut firmly behind him.

Mona and von Stilicho did not speak to one another. They retired to her room for a short session of angry and almost satisfying love-making — all of this accomplished without either person saying much of anything. The Chevalier, as always, rolled over but, this time, before falling to sleep, he seemed to think twice and, surprisingly, tried a couple things that, although clumsily performed, at least conveyed a certain baseline consideration for his sometime lover and attorney.

And then he fell asleep.

Mona could not.

She rose around 3 a.m. and threw on a robe. She filled a cup with water, sipped it, and quietly stepped into the hall.

The castle was quiet and dark, the candelabra having burned down in the night, but running lights along the floor — as might show the way to an emergency exit in a Japanese hotel — led her to where she wanted to go.

The fire had almost died in the trophy room. It was cold now, damply so. Mona pulled tight on the lapels of the robe, hugging herself. Had there been a pack of cigarettes, she'd have smoked one. Instead she plopped down on Donovan's throne and thought.

What struck her above all was the wild-eyed passion with which he evangelized his nation. Only his nation. He had never once spoken of policy — of taxes or budgets, environmental concerns, foreign commitments, welfare or laissez faire, anything like that. In all Donovan's ramblings, there had been no talk of the state, except insofar as his open hostility to law and the Constitution implied a certain contempt for all such formal structures. The power of the state — which

94

the President and his supporters currently possessed — and over which Donovan professed to exercise the ultimate influence, was to him, it seemed, as he called it, a mere instrumentality.

Donovan was using the President, somehow, to create or resurrect a nation. And Mona France still did not understand how or why.

She didn't feel at all tired.

She scanned the bookshelves but found only musty military histories, illustrated atlases of various wars, and Bicentennial-era coffee table books depicting a longer-haired, more bell-bottomed version of Americana. She inspected the knickknacks on the mantlepiece but could not seem to find the beauty in the snow globe — it wasn't even snow, but a kind of silvery confetti — that had entranced von Stilicho. The framed maps on the wall depicted obscure midwestern counties as they'd looked perhaps a hundred years ago, but provided none of the deeper answers that Mona France sought. As for the empty stares of the severed cow heads lining the wall — had one or two actually been added in the time they'd been here? — she avoided these as best she could.

At last she inspected the statute on the end table, heretofore alluded to but not described. This was of Atreus preparing to finish off his nemesis with the sword of Dedaelus, et cetera. It was silver, well-proportioned, but altogether too fluid in its lines, as though, instead of depicting solid creatures in mortal combat, it was simply about to melt. And then Mona noticed:

Atreus' arm wasn't quite of a piece with his body. There was a seam at the shoulder. As if it were on a pivot.

She inspected this closely, concluded that it was, and — applying minimal pressure — and then a bit more when it failed to budge — twisted it.

The arm lowered.

And the panel in the wall opened.

Mona hesitated not a moment. She drew the belt of the robe tighter, re-knotted it, and entered the labyrinth.

ODOACER

The floor was made up of cobble-stones, polished clean and black in the center, well-travelled, dustier on the edges. It was lit by dim blue lights, spaced at roughly 20-foot intervals. And it was cold, very cold.

Mona moved briskly.

After 100 feet, a small passageway veered to the right. It consisted of three steps and, at the top, a dark window. She climbed the former and pressed her head to the latter. With a start, Mona France recognized the now-familiar form of her room, and the still more familiar form of von Stilicho sleeping on the bed with a content grin. She was seeing it all, darkly now, through the other side of the mirror. Of that she was sure. Had Donovan been watching her, she wondered with disgust, and what had he seen?

She resumed the main corridor and continued on her way.

The perverted little peepholes were all over the place. Through the backs of mirrors, ventilation grates, cracks in the wall, and eyeholes cut in old portraits, the tunnels offered views of nearly every corner of the castle: the dining hall, the parlour, the billiard room, et cetera. The location and aspect of these places were all old news to Mona France, but there were new discoveries as well.

Through another mirror, she found herself inspecting a spartan barracks housing exactly 20 beds. In the nearest of these she discerned the unmistakable features of a sleeping Proud-boy and assumed the rising and falling lumps in the others were Proud-boys too.

Through another she caught her first glimpse of the hypothesized but heretofore unseen garage. It was a giant, regular, rectangular space lit by banks of fluorescent lamps. There were ten, twelve, maybe thirteen land vehicles, six of which were antique or novelty cars — but the rest of which struck Mona France as practical escape vehicles, should the opportunity arise. The inevitable Bentley in English Racing Green, the inevitable red Ferrari — and, should the need for force arise — a camouflaged HUM-V and what looked like a

ODOACER

tank. At the far end of the structure, under what looked like a circular aperture in the roof, rested a helicopter and, Mona noted with dread — having come to know Ritter von Stilicho's predilections so well — a deflated hot air balloon.

Mona made a mental note of all this and continued on her way. After a couple hours of exploring the tunnels, she could see the milky-pale light of morning filtering through the windows of the rooms she observed. Soon Chateau Trois-Fois-Maître would be awake and buzzing — perhaps buzzing was not the word — but alive with the silent, loping machinations of the Proud-boys. She was about to turn around when, reaching a new bend in the path, she felt the cool tickle of a breeze on her neck. Ten paces further she found its source: a door, left ajar.

Silently she edged up to the crack and peered in. She had never seen this room before. It was large, but barely furnished, with an enormous bank of windows along the far wall. The blinds were pulled on these. The furnishing consisted of a single enormous canopy bed, piled high with blankets and cushions and — save for one distinctly Peter Donovan-sized clearing in the middle — covered in an astonishing array of porcelain Victorian dolls and stuffed animals.

But the Lord of Trois-Fois-Maître was not there.

Now it was definitely time to go, Mona concluded. But she could not go just yet. There was, mere paces from the door to Donovan's private apartment, a final alcove. This one was dusty, strewn with cobwebs, but, like the others, it afforded access to a peephole. Mona peeped.

And she thereby discovered Donovan's control room.

Analog clocks displayed the time in various world cities. The local time — three hours behind New York — confirmed that they were on the west coast. Lite-brite-style monitors appeared to be tracking satellites in sine-curve orbits along mercator projections of the world. Telephones, many telephones. An oversized world map lay on a large conference table, pierced hundreds of times with what appeared to be color-coded pins of some sort. Directly opposite her was a large, dark monitor faced by a large, modern swivel chair with an array of nobs and buttons on the armrest. There were many other screens besides — a whole bank of them, flickering silently. And, finally, to the right of those, a monitor opened to the President's Twitter page.

A cursor hung in wait over a blank text box.

A toilet flushed and the Lord of Trois-Fois-Maître entered and positioned himself in the throne. He was dressed for the day in yet another muumuu — this one striped gold and a metallic red — with a large cubit zarconian pendant dangling over his chest, and as always the crystal tiara.

After stretching and taking a sip of something, Donovan rubbed his hands together and and began eying the bank of monitors embedded in the console before him. They were oddly old-fashioned, with bulging, convex screens displaying grainy black-and-white images. Most depicted dark rooms — as far as she could tell, one was a barber shop, closed for the night, another a diner, just opening and mostly empty, another what could have been the rec room in a church basement, a dining room, a den, a locker room, and so on. Donovan appeared to be watching one screen with particular interest. This showed a bar — whitewashed, too bright to be cozy, with neon beer lamps. Three men were awake and talking. Donovan jiggled a knob on the armrest that, Mona assumed, controlled the volume.

"I can't stand that fucking kid," came one tinny voice.

"You're drunk, dude," came another.

"You can't say that, dude."

"Why?"

"Cause those kids got shot."

"Fuck it, that kid's a douche."

"Dude."

"Look, let's just be cool, okay?"

"How about this — okay? It's one thing to have to go through something like that. But that doesn't mean you can just take away other people's rights."

ODOACER

"Well, yeah. But maybe we should be open to other things. Like getting the real crazy kids before they — well."

Donovan muted the sound and hunched over a keyboard. Mona watched in astonishment as letters and then fully-formed words leapt across the President's open Twitter account on the next monitor. There were some false starts, some word-smithing and erasures, but in a matter of moments, these words came out — "I salute the brave students who are speaking up to make our schools safer. All options must be on the table, including mental health monitoring, which we can do consistently with our sacred duty to uphold our inviolable Second Amendment rights." —and then were posted.

Donovan leaned back, cradling his immense head in interwoven fingers.

There was a flicker on the screen as the little gray men reached into their pockets and pulled out their phones, and then as they appeared to exchange high-fives.

Donovan emitted a short guffaw and resumed typing. This time, after a burst of activity and then a few meditative edits, he wrote: "therefore I am hereby ordering the Commerce Secretary to investigate raising tariffs on Canadian pork products." The former presidential advisor reread this, changed "pork" to "poultry" and then "Canadian" to "Spanish" — all this with a quiet, heaving, healthy, mirthful chuckle — and then turned again to the bank of Space Age closed-circuit monitors. He toggled the sound, listening to the audio from first one monitor, then another, as he cast about for Mona knew not what.

The bar had shut down. The church basement was still empty. The barber had opened for the day and was cutting an older man's hair, but the conversation concerned a ballgame. The diner was full, and it seemed Donovan had the ability to redirect the mic: the folks at one table were talking about their Mexican server, who they though was being deliberately slow, the man at the counter was grumbling into his phone something about pest control, and how goddamn expensive it was. Neither these nor any of the other

ODOACER

conversations at the diner, seemed to be exactly what Donovan was looking for. He shook his head, muttering "come on people," then fixated on a screen showing what appeared to be a breakfast nook.

Here, an older white man in a flannel shirt hunched over a table reading a local newspaper. A younger woman, probably his daughter, fried something — eggs — on the grill and tried, haltingly, to make conversation with what was obviously a very grouchy and unpleasant old man.

"Did you see about the fire department? I thought that was great."

The old man grunted.

"I kept telling them they just had to have a bake sale or something."

"Fucking thieves," growled the old man.

"Oh, they're okay."

"What was wrong with the old truck?"

"It was old."

And so it went — more often than not punctuated by long and angry silences — until the daughter asked the unbearable old man what he was reading.

"Goddamn county government is screwing us again. Do they think we were born yesterday?"

"Oh."

Donovan shut off the sound and started typing the predicate to the order regarding Swedish poultry products. This came out, with additional reworking, as "Unfair trade deals are screwing this country again. Our trading partners have for too long thought we were stupid — and they were right! I am changing that. I am therefore ordering the Commerce Secretary to investigate raising tariffs on Spanish poultry products."

"Spanish" was at the last moment replaced by "Portuguese," "to investigate raising tariffs" was changed to "to irrevocably raise tariffs," and the tweet was sent.

Donovan turned the sound back on.

The daughter picked her phone off the counter and read the screen.

"What?" asked the old man.

"The President."

"What'd he say?"

The daughter extended the phone to the old man. He held his head askance, like he had trouble reading the letters, and then burst out in a hard laugh.

"Damn," the old man said. "He's kicking some ass. At last."

Astonished by what she'd seen — almost too astonished to breathe — Mona France at last paid heed to the hour and scurried in a panic back to the trophy room and, finally, unseen — as far as she could tell — to her room.

The Chevalier was just waking up. "Ah, good morning, love," he said. "Have you been up for a while?"

CHAPTER SIXTEEN

PROUD PAPA

It was the kind of reflective awareness that, in you or me, would regard itself as driving the whole show — as though its thoughts were *sui generis* the original and necessary principle from which all the body's actions flowed: a soul. But in its case — that is to say, in the case of the awareness — with a self-critical wisdom not usually attributed to its putative owner, it had recognized its subservience to the tangle of impulses, drives and responses that commanded action, action, action.

It did not know these personally. It thought of them as a "Them," and for all it knew They had their own awarenesses. But if They did, They were strangers to it. It knew Them only by their works. These had once been felt: the heat, the rising blood at the back, the giddy euphoria in the shoulders and neck, the void in the stomach, the *thumos*, the *phrenes*, the *noos*. But the feeling had gone away as it gradually relinquished any pretext of being an equal partner in whatever kind of joint venture it had entered with Them. Now it was an observer.

ODOACER

It was, despite appearances, almost perfectly self-aware — and with perfect self-awareness it had sealed itself hermetically in its little cell to contemplate life and death and its own mysterious origins. Whatever made it made the rest of the man too, made Them, and it was humbled in the presence of its creator. Humility: another word seldom associated with the man. It surrendered completely to whatever plan had been devised for it. It prayed.

None of this was to say They never let it out. They in their wisdom recognized there were times when only it could speak convincingly. For instance, when it spoke of the children, whom it pitied with compassion, disgust and guilt. The kids, they were Theirs. It had been, perhaps not by its own choosing, an absentee parent through their childhoods. And They had raised the babies, for better or for worse. And the children bore Their stamp. And it loved and hated Them for it. So They would give it the microphone, let it say a word or two about the children, always keeping it on a short leash. It didn't matter that it was so out of practice the words came out wrong, expressed in a language of thought as much as a language of speech. The evident sincerity was what counted. And then it would be released from service, to return, gratefully, to its cell and to its prayer.

Today, one of the elder sons was standing in a small, dingy office with the man. Never mind which son. It had ceased distinguishing them. The office was typical of a government office, living concrete testimony to the modern view that taxpayer dollars should be spent only on ugly things. There was a window which looked out onto an airshaft, but in any event was covered by venetian blinds that — but for certain irregular and very noticeably hideous kinks in their alignment — purported to be closed. Cheap faux-wood paneling extended about shoulder-high from the floor, and the rest was slathered in an awful lime-green paint. Two desks, each steel, yet straining under the weight of an outmoded computer, a fan, a mini fridge. There was a bulletin board, a couple maps — though the import of these, and their relation to the office's mission, were not immediately obvious. There were not pictures or personal effects on the desks, just stacks of paperwork.

The man had been deposited here, briefly, before a scheduled address to the staff of whatever agency was housed in this office. It did not know which, and was fairly sure They did not know either, but whatever banalities the man read would, given luck, be hailed as suitably Presidential.

The son fidgeted. His suit fit much better than the man's, almost to the point of slickness, and this went with his hair, which was also slick. The son retracted his upper lip, as if to liberate some particle of uneaten lunch from his gum, then stole a first nervous glance at his father. And then another one.

"Try to stand still for once," barked the man.

The son straightened and adjusted his thin tie with a gesture that was calculated — poorly — to come off as purposeful.

"I said stop. I didn't say fondle your tie."

"Sorry dad."

The man snorted.

"Dad?"

The man took a step toward the door, opened it a crack and peered through. This let in the not terribly thunderous din of the civil servants in the next room. They were reportedly demoralized over something the man had done and needed a pep talk. Or, in any event, they were deemed to need to be seen receiving a pep talk.

"Dad?"

"What?"

The man sat on the edge of a desk and unbuttoned his coat, which, although baggy when he stood, was stretched by the compacting girth of the man's abdomen.

"Did you mean what you said in that tweet this morning."

It felt around it a sudden rush. Neck-hairs on end, eyebrows alert, a burning in the stomach and chest, a tenseness in the hands, which contorted into claws. Breath poured heavily in and out of the man's nose and mouth.

The man had not read tweets this morning.

"Of course I meant it," the man barked.

The son's eyes opened wide and his head shook, briefly, in narrowing oscillations like a spring coming to rest. He smiled. "Really, dad?"

The man snorted and looked away. "God damn it," the man said, addressing the son by name. "You think I just throw bullshit our there to be ignored?"

"No, dad," answered the son with a visible gulp. "It's just a figure of speech. What I mean to say is thank you." He took a step closer to his father and raised his hands, just about hip height, in a gesture that would have been an invitation to hug were it not so briskly rejected.

"Alright. Don't be a f——." (The President must be presidential, but we shall choose our words in reporting his.)

"Okay," said the son. "Thanks, dad."

It later learned that the President's son was thereby appointed chair to an administratively insignificant, but nonetheless high profile select commission that had been tasked with investigating the role of marijuana in mass shootings.

The door then opened and three secret service agents entered. They escorted the man to the assembled bureaucrats who, despite the promised pep talk, offered only polite applause.

It felt the shoulders tighten and the nostrils flare.

CHAPTER SEVENTEEN

EZIO IS A TREE-HUGGER

Charles awoke early and rode his bike to the riverbank in predawn gloom. He lived close by, and his plan was to arrive before the guys and hide the bike, lest they deem it inauthentic. He was surprised, then, and a little nervous, to find that Ezio had gotten there before him.

The unofficial leader of the unofficial Benice's chapter of the unofficial Red Hats of America leaned against the front bumper of his truck, pouring coffee from a plaid thermos into a styrofoam cup. He wore rubber waders and, under them, a heavy shirt. He'd forebear his red cap, today, in favor of an old, brown number, much stained, that was undoubtedly lucky in some way. He watched the steam rise off the river, which was narrow and muddy, and bent in an almost perfect U that enclosed the dirt parking lot on three sides. Along the edges were patches of gravel from which low, light green bushes sprouted.

Ezio squinted as the sun came up, strengthening the impression given by the sharp vertical creases that ran from his cheeks to his chin, and of the vaguely slavic jawline that fanned out in wide triangles below each of his knobby, ruddy cheeks.

He spotted Charles and smiled.

"Morning, 'migo," he said. "Can I fix you some coffee?"

Charles hopped off the bike and walked it over to the other man. "Sure," he said. "Got milk?"

"Cream," Ezio responded, fishing a couple little disposable containers — the kind given out at cheap restaurants — from a small cooler chest. "Have a seat."

It was a big pickup truck, marketed to men like Ezio who responded to the bundles of associations — like "strong promises," "rock," and what not — featured in the TV ads. Ezio had his late wife's name painted on the fender, roughly where a ship's name would be, and the letters filled with the color pattern of the American flag. THEKLA was therefore the truck's name, all capitalized, full of patriotism. Pink breast cancer ribbons flanked it.

Charles found a spot on the bumper and stirred the cream into his coffee.

"Nice bike," said Ezio, nodding toward the conveyance.

"Yes," Charles responded tentatively. "Well, I gotta. Fucking DUI. You understand."

Ezio chuckled. "Well, it's a great way to get around," he said. "I got one myself. Sometimes ride it on the weekends, just to clear out my head. That's a little Andrew, I suppose but, well — I like it."

Charles said nothing, but the men exchanged smiles.

"There're some pretty good trails around here, 'specially up in the hills." He sipped his coffee. "Maybe we should go up there sometime?"

"Sure," Charles said. "I'd like that."

Neither spoke for several minutes as the sun rose over the hills, probably the same hills. A fish or two leapt out of the water and flopped back in. A truck rumbled by on the road and then droned off into the distance. The air was chilly and rough on the lungs.

"Goddamn," said Ezio at last. "I love it out here."

Charles tensed. This was an Interest, a True Interest, unlike all those other interests he'd seen in the bar, on the street, and everywhere else. He saw this as an opening — he'd need to be delicate.

"Yes," he said. "I hope it's around forever."

"Oh sure," Ezio responded, smiling broadly. "It will be. It will be."

Charles shook his head. "Ezio?"

"Yeah?"

"You ever wonder if this global warming hoax is — maybe — real? I saw this guy on TV who —"

Ezio exhaled, blowing a flutter of hot air up into his own eyes and nose. "Yeah, Charles. I guess it is."

"It is?"

"Yeah. I think so."

Charles was not expecting this. "How do you suppose we deal with it?" He asked at length. "And what about the water and all that?"

Ezio thought a moment. "Yeah," he said. "Yeah, that's a problem."

Again there was silence — or comparative silence. A bird cooed, another bird squawked. Someone, somewhere, pretty far off, had switched on some kind of motorized farm equipment. The water in the river trickled by in its own quiet way.

Ezio exhaled loudly, grabbed his device from his pocket and stared. Then he smiled, reassured, and gave Charles a gentle punch on the shoulder.

"It's him," he said.

He held the device aloft and read to Charles: "Park Service is safeguarding America's most precious assets. We must preserve our natural splendor for future Americans!"

Ezio seemed lost.

"You okay?" Charles asked.

ODOACER

"Yeah," said Ezio. "Just thinking."

"I mean, I guess that's great," said Charles. "But —"

He flinched slightly and gripped his device.

Ezio shook his head and took a step away from THEKLA. Then he again stared at his screen, heaved a sigh of relief, and read the substance of the message to Charles Earl Jarlsberg III.

This one had a different message, something about football and football players. The President said that a certain quarterback lacked patriotism and that his distantly remembered protests were direct and intended insults to the soldiers, sailors and marines who, evidently, fought and died that a national symbol may be worshipped according to formula. And it was an insult to him, the President. Ezio read this very slowly and clearly: "It is an insult to me, his President, who wants to keep him safe." The President then went on to suggest — in language evocative of certain unfashionable theories of labor relations — that the NFL owners should prevent "their" players from engaging in similar protests.

Ezio grinned, half embarrassed, half thrilled.

"God, it's kinda exhausting," he said.

"Yes?" Charles prompted him.

"But it's got to be said by someone. The flag, the troops. I mean, someone's got to say it, right?"

Charles did not say it.

"The dignity of the office."

Charles looked away.

Ezio's lower jaw dropped and he stammered a moment. "I mean, I mean —"

He again stared into the screen — "another," he said — and again read to Charles.

"America's heritage," he read, "will always be protected" — Ezio emphasized this word — "by the brave men and women of our national park system. Happy birthday, NPS!"

"Well," said Ezio at last.

109

ODOACER

"Well," repeated Charles dreamily. "I think it's a 'service.'"

"I mean, you saw what he wrote," persisted Ezio, not really caring if it was one thing or the other, or whether Charles had read it.

"Yes, you told me."

Ezio stroked his chin and stared solemnly at the onrushing waters. "I mean, he cares — he really cares — about us. And he will protect us — all this." He gestured vaguely at the splendor of it all.

"Okay," said Charles dejectedly.

"And the parks."

Charles Earl Jarlsberg III sighed. "I suppose."

"Well," said Ezio. "One thing at a time. We'll fix it. We'll fix it all. He cares."

The fishing was good. Charles didn't catch anything, but in spite of everything he had fun with Ezio and the rest of the guys. He'd gotten too drunk and forgotten his bike, taking a ride home instead. He'd realized that halfway, but decided not to mention it. He still wasn't sure how the rest of the guys would react to the bike.

When he got home, he checked his phone. The President had been on Twitter, of course, but Charles didn't see any of the tweets Ezio had read out to him.

Must have been a bug, he thought. And he went to sleep.

CHAPTER EIGHTEEN

THE MAN WHO SOLD THE WORLD

The man was watching television. He was watching three televisions, but only one had sound. It was 10 in the morning. The chief of staff waited two doors down with the morning business, the details of which had been worked out in a series of meetings and the output of which now required the man's signature.

The room was white, light and airy, even with the loose-knit cotton curtains drawn over the bank of wide, double-paned windows on the south side. The furniture was light and white too, including the overstuffed leather sofa on which the man now sat, somewhat stooped, with his arms splayed out along the back, crucifixion style, and his overlong red tie hanging low over his crotch. As usual, the man had kept his suit jacket on.

The program with the sound on was a morning show hosted by a panel of three of the man's most sycophantic fans, any two of whom could have served as the *baka-tarento*, and the third of whom — it could be anyone, depending on the circumstances — defaulted into the relative role of world-

111

weary sobriety personified. The topic, as so often was the case, was the morning's tweets. These had been threatening and, on balance, at least according to the other newscasters, jarring to constitutional order, but in their own way they back-tracked on certain comments that had been made the previous evening that — as happened from time to time — had spurred certain retiring members of this or that congressional caucus to offer vague expressions of dismay and concern.

Specifically, the man had responded off-handedly to a soft-ball question from the press pool as he walked from the lectern. The softball question had been: "Do you condemn the theft of the Cape Town Sapphire and what steps is the FBI taking to find the perpetrators?" The off-handed response had been: "You know — it's a terrible thing. This emerald. The thing is, not many people know, the emerald belongs to America. And there are a lot of lies out there — a lot of lies — about who owns it, a lot of fake news — but the emerald, it's America's emerald. And my predecessor, who will go nameless — America has been humiliated. Terrible negotiations, worst ever. And, now, you see, we're getting our honor back. And I'm doing what — I'm restoring. And people are seeing that countries aren't pushing around America anymore. And, you know, a lot of people are waking up to that. And things are changing big-league — with South Africa, and with lots of places, a lot of places — and America. Believe me." And the reporter asked, in follow up, a softball follow-up question: "And what about the FBI, sir? Are they investigating this matter?" And the off-handed response was: "Well, things are really changing in the FBI now. Big improvement in morale. America's police. They are brave men (and women — most people don't know that), keeping us safe. And that hasn't always been the case. Justice department was politicized. Terrible. Really terrible. A tremendous scandal. Not getting reported by fake news, but. The people responsible — will be held accountable. There's no question about that. Came after me with fake, fake — this nonsense. This Russia nonsense. But that's changing now." And a

ODOACER

softball follow-up to that softball follow-up: "Mr. President, are they investigating the theft of the Cape Town Sapphire." And the man had off-handedly shrugged his shoulders, said "it's America's emerald and we've fixed that," and strolled away.

It had wondered after these pronouncements if They were taking things on a course that would end in prison. It wasn't completely horrified by this thought. Maybe, in prison, They would let it read. They would let it read over the little passage of Melville that it read at the event, and that it — for it had one of the all-time-great memories, don't you know? — had memorized.

But it knew it was fooling itself. They would not let it read. They would not go to prison and, even if They did, the man would still be a hero. They would rage from behind bars, and enrage, and keep the message alive — They would find their medium. And at the first hiccup, the first foreign humiliation or economic downturn, the people — not all of them, but many of them — would wonder what all the fuss had been about anyhow, and remember how things seemed better back then, and curse the politicized prosecution of one whose only crime had been — what, really? Was any of this even criminal?

And, raging, They would be remembered and, raging, They would be rehabilitated. And it would never get to read *Moby-Dick* anyway. So, rather than allow itself to get carried away on such absurd flights of fancy, it contemplated its creator and prayed.

And then the tweets had come in the morning and cleared things up — but not really. These said: "The theft of the Cape Town Emerald, which is and has always been U.S. property, will be investigated by my FBI." And: "I have ordered my FBI chief to investigate entire matter, including corrupt process by which emerald was handed over to South Africa. #Bribes #Sellout" And: "If any wrongdoing is found, including illegal and Unethical dealings with South Africa, prosecutions will be instigated. #Sellout" And: "Emerald

113

ODOACER

should never have been given away by corrupt administration. Real crime here is to America." And: "The TRUTH will get out."

These had triggered a flurry of hand-wringing on the morning shows and across the internet. If the statements the night before had suggested the man might have, at the very least, been complicit in, or supportive of, what amounted to an international jewel heist, and had no intention of using the FBI as anything but a foil, the morning's tweets had at least changed the narrative. To wit, the President wanted the matter investigated, but the *whole* matter, including the affront to national dignity arising from the ceding of the jewel to South Africa in the first place. The tweet's suggestion that this had been the result of a corrupt process had, almost in and of itself, created the conditions for officially investigating that process as the only proper course of action — at least among that very considerable portion of the commentariat that proceeded in its labors on the insurmountable assumption that the President of the United States of America didn't simply say, or write, whatever bullshit popped into his head. So the story now was that the President wasn't just having the FBI investigate *part* of the story — that is, the actual, physical theft of an allied sovereign state's national treasure — but the *whole* story, including the many wrongs done to the America, and whatever nefarious machinations on the part of the man's political rivals may have led to them.

But the tweets had made waves, too, in their own way. Some twitter commentators and journalists had the nerve to suggest that the accusations vis-à-vis the previous administration were completely baseless and irresponsible, and that the man was creating a public outcry, among his most feverish supporters, out of whole cloth, in order to foster general confusion and cynicism. Others — unfairly and, as a matter of public perception, pointlessly — reconstructed in pain-staking and meticulous detail the history of the Cape Town Sapphire — or Emerald if the President wanted it to be an emerald — the murky series of transactions that brought it

ODOACER

to the United States, and the complex diplomatic framework for its return. Still other commentators objected to the use of terms like "my FBI" and the chief executive's hands-on, and rather personal, approach to directing the field operations of the national police force — which they peevishly suggested amounted to an unprecedented concentration of presidential power that eroded agency independence and politicized law enforcement.

Oh, They had roiled at all that nastiness. But They'd only watched it briefly before turning to the morning panel with the three drooling sycophants, who put the world right again. The chyron alternated "Sell-out on Cape Town Emerald" and "President Orders Investigation of Wrongdoing in Cape Town Give-Away." One of the three — the older guy — was at this very moment, praising the President's magnanimity of spirit: the emerald (it was an emerald, to hell with it) matter would be investigated in a manner that would be fair to all sides, let the chips fall where they may. How could everyone, from all sides, not be happy with this development? And the younger guy added that, given how serious the allegations about the previous administration were, it only made sense to investigate these along with the so-called theft itself.

And They calmed. They cooled. It could barely feel Them. Breathing slowed. The world became foggy, almost pixelated. A swirl of color and beauty.

Once again, the tweets had saved the operation. The tweets had saved the operation from Them. And the tweets had saved Them from Themselves.

It tried to remember how all this started.

It had already found peace and connectedness to all things. That is to say, it was already outside of time at the time. It was not paying close attention to significant things outside, and little at the time indicated this would be significant. It was just — weird. But in time it and They had become, if not resigned to things — They never resigned —

115

ODOACER

then willing to ally with a secret new friend. A secret new and wonderful friend.

It was — though it didn't really think in years — around the beginning of the man's predecessor's term. It was innocuous. An announcement, attributed to the man, that the man would appear on a late night show. They barely paid attention. If anything, it drove ratings and They loved that. The tweets drew attention to the operation. The tweets made the operation cutting edge. The tweets were a direct, unfiltered, unmediated link between the man and the man's public. It was more bothered by the tweets than They were. It felt it odd and disconcerting that They weren't in control — but maybe it was Them. Maybe it wasn't paying attention.

A few years later, the tweets became more aggressive. Attacks on the predecessor, on his competence, on his deal-making, or on his proclaimed willingness to get played by foe and ally alike in the name of an illusory and disadvantageous peace. On the dishonor he had brought to America. Of the shame. Of how things didn't feel the way they used to feel, and how that was his fault.

They noticed.

They noticed because the initial press was negative. It was not that the detractors accused the man of breaching decorum, speaking out of turn, being ill-informed, or pandering to this or that segment of the sewer system. It was that they painted the man as ridiculous, and They no doubt understood that there were versions of the world in which that was true. In which the man was a has-been, an almost-ran, a puff of hot air. An absurd, needy, ignorant, foolish figure. A laughing-stock. The butt of jokes in any club to whose membership he aspired. The tweets called attention to the man in an unflattering way — or, more accurately, in a way that all but invited others, the man's detractors and enemies, to paint him in unflattering ways, or to agree, and to think, that the absurd figure in the painting was the real man.

It remembered the day They exploded. Dr. Freundhein was there.

ODOACER

It was in New York. Or maybe in Florida. It all looked the same inside.

Dr. Freundhein examined the man. Nothing intrusive. The man wouldn't be poked or prodded. The man wouldn't ever undress. And the man insisted on reporting his height and weight. But Freundhein was allowed to shine a light in the man's ears and up his nose, and to have the man say ahh while Freundhein inspected the man's tonsils. Reflex tests, one on each knee, demanded a light touch, and were thus administered, and the man's reflexes were proclaimed excellent, unprecedented, the best ever.

The man must have looked sad or distracted, not been his usual self. For Freundhein asked:

"Boss," he said, "I got to ask. You look down. Is something bothering you?"

The man had stared at the doctor for a long time. The doctor stared back, warmly, coaxingly. However the man looked at him — and it could only assume this was done with the menacing scowl reserved for all uninvited intimacies — the doctor held his gaze and, with a benevolent and almost ridiculous expression on his grizzled, disheveled round face, waited the man out.

"Doc," said the man at last, "I'm just pissed. Did you see some of the stuff the press has been saying about me?"

The good doctor nodded sagely, stroking his chingristle with fine, thin fingers. "I'm afraid I don't follow the news so closely, boss." He smiled breezily and brushed a speck of dust off his patient's be-suited shoulder. "My advice, don't worry so much what people have to say. There will always be critics."

The man again said nothing for a period. They must have been calculating things — turning phrase — figuring out how to say They feared looking ridiculous without acknowledging the possibility of that ever happening — either to the doctor or to themselves — either the looking ridiculous or the fear of it. It knew Them well.

117

ODOACER

"They're attacking me because of what I'm saying on Twitter, doc. But, you know, someone's got to say it. Someone's got to stand up for."

The man didn't complete the sentence. He moved on to the next.

"And it's unfair. So unfair. Because they just go after, whatever. It doesn't even matter whether what you say. They attack. It's personal. They make it personal. They lie. And they make it."

Again, the man started in on the next thought before completing the last.

"It's not my fault, doc. It's true. But, you know."

The doctor leaned forward and his expression became ominously dark. A parrot shrieked through the open window and a warm, wet breeze came in with the noise. Florida — it must have been in Florida. The doctor leaned in and said, "what do you mean, boss, that it's not your fault?"

The man again said nothing, this time for what seemed like many, many long seconds. It could feel Them raging next to it, flooding around it on both sides, over and under it, rushing to the front of the face, to the eyes and nose and to the mouth, where They could do the most damage. But the man remained modulated.

"I stand by everything I say, doc. Everything. Every word of it."

The doctor nodded.

"Even if I don't say it, doc, I stand by what I say. I don't blink. You see? I don't back down, I don't give up. I don't get butt-fucked."

The doctor winced a bit at the metaphor, but generally held his ground.

"But, you know, doc? Sometimes I feel — sometimes I feel."

Again, the man was silent for a time.

And then it felt itself floating forward, settling in the neck, filling up the larynx. It felt breath, going in cold and

ODOACER

going out hot. It saw the world, briefly, through blinkering eyes.

"Sometimes I feel like I'm not in control, Doc."

And then it felt itself rushing back, exhilarated, to wherever it belonged — to the center of the universe, to the epicenter of the Bag Bang, to the beginning, and end, of space and time. That They were raging furious about it hardly made an impression, They were so far away.

But there, so far away, the scene continued.

The doctor nodded. He smiled kindly.

"I think I understand what you're telling me, boss."

"You do?" asked the man.

"Yes," said the doctor. "I've had experience with this kind of thing before. I get it. It's not a medical matter strictly speaking. But it has a medical effect. It has a medical effect, and so I must know about it, and treat it. I can make inquiries." The doctor spied the man under arched eyebrows, head slightly askew, then added, "discreet, very discreet inquiries. I have people who know people — who are good at this. We can beat this."

After the doctor had taken leave that time, all was quiet. It lasted a good many months. Then the tweets about the predecessor's birthplace started. And the man looked ridiculous again, or could be portrayed that way. This time, the man called Freundhein to his office on Fifth Avenue.

The man sat behind a heavy, dark-wood desk, set on a little pedestal, and stared down on the grizzly little doctor in the long white lab coat, who fidgeted on the marble-tiled floor below.

"Freundhein," said the man. "Remember when we talked a few months back about — tweets?"

The doctor nodded vigorously and appeared to regain his composure.

"You said you'd look into it."

"Yes, boss. I did."

"Did you find anything out?" asked the man.

"I did," said the doctor.

119

ODOACER

"And what did you find out?"

"I have made — contact. I have made contact with someone who is." He paused. "Someone who is credible. Who has, on a few occasions now, proved some connection to the. To the. To the matter."

The man leaned forward, his head low over the desk and his hands folded just under his chin.

"Who is it?"

"I don't know, boss. They talk to me. Only me. I don't dare tell anyone else. All I can say is, they are admirers. They are fans of yours. They want you to succeed. And."

"And?" said the man. The voice was not angry. Not angry at all. It was pleased. It was grateful. It was the voice the used when presented with a business opportunity. Assured, charming, the voice of your best friend. Or the voice of a scary guy who could be your best friend, now that he's convinced you're the real thing. A voice that makes you feel special, smart, onto something.

"And, boss, they have asked me to be their contact person."

The doctor took a step closer toward the desk.

"They say that you can call me anytime you need to reach them. With any message you want to give them."

Another step closer.

"They say they are your friend."

CHAPTER NINETEEN

MR. ROGERS' NEIGHBORHOOD

The guys were in a sentimental way.

The barbecue was the first even semi-official political event that Charles had attended with the guys, and semi-official may have been overstating the case. It was a barbecue, in Obie's backyard, to celebrate Obie's birthday, but it had been given a patriotic theme that at least resonated politically. There had been flags on the invitation and there were flags and bunting in the yard. The invitation had made a vague allusion to the troops, none of whom were in attendance, but who were, in some way, being celebrated: the "Support our Troops" and "Land of the Free Because of the Brave" lawn signs confirmed and effectuated this. And then there was the ever-present commander-in-chief, whose sage, scowling visage appeared on the invitation and whose spirit, as always, hung over everything. So it was that Charles Earl Jarlsberg III, knowing the guys were political but not political, organized but not organized, engaged but not engaged, thought of this as a semi-official event.

Charles arrived at 5. Obie's was a townhouse in a subdivision south of town. His was the two-story one nestled

ODOACER

between two three-story units, and the interior easily betrayed his single lifestyle: cheap furniture, scant decoration, a bookshelf full of video games and DVDs. The guests were hustled past this and Obie's almost empty kitchenette on their ways to the barbecue in the back.

It was warm, without a breeze, but the trees — a grove of which grew just over the property line in a ravine — had blossomed, providing some shade in the modest-sized yard. By seven, it was deemed that all the guys who would be there were there, and there were six guys there: Kasey, Obie, Chris, Ken, Scott, Dan, and Charles Earl Jarlsberg III. The ones with wives, girlfriends, kids and the like had stayed away, except for Kasey, who'd brought his ten-year-old, Brianna.

Charles mused sourly that the event was, as a political rally, a bust. And so far it hadn't even been fun, not even by the guys' depressive and mean-spirited standards. And he missed Ezio, who has home with a sick child.

Obie had started the coals at 4:30 and they'd burned out by 6. He was on the third set at 7:30 when the burgers — store-bought frozen patties — were finally cooking. The guys huddled about the chef, drinking beer. And they were, it should be said again, in a sentimental way.

"Do you remember when this used to be a farm?" asked Kasey.

"Yes," said Chris. "I do, as a matter of fact. Treat Farms."

"Tree-Eat Farms," Ken shot in. "You could pick apples."

"Yeah, that's it."

"All this stuff is new," Kasey continued, nursing his beer.

"Town's changed a lot."

"Not for the better."

"Definitely not for the better."

Obie flipped the burgers. "It's not so bad." There was a tweak of hostility in his tone. He was very proud of the house, which he'd bought with the proceeds of his oft-talked-

ODOACER

about, never-described business. "It's a good community. Good schools."

Kasey shot a glance at Brianna, seated at the picnic table, who had taken her father's cell phone early in the evening and now was dead to the world.

"Bri, I want that phone back at some point," Kasey said without conviction.

"Fine. Later."

"It's not good for you."

"I'm bored," she pouted.

"Fine, just ten more minutes, okay?"

The child dissolved again into the device, having no firm concept of ten minutes except insofar as she knew it would not be ten minutes.

"When did it change?" Scott exclaimed.

"Not all at once," was Dan's response. "It happened while we weren't paying attention. Used to be you walked down Main Street and everyone you saw."

The guys nodded.

"People were helpful."

"You knew them."

"You knew their families."

"The music was better."

And so on.

Kasey then blurted out: "You know what it was like? It was like Mr. Rogers."

He meant the children's show.

The guys paused, sipped their drinks, and waited to hear the rest of his theory.

Kasey seemed unsure of what to say. "Bri?"

"Dad, I'm watching something."

"How's it like Mr. Rogers, Kase?"

Kasey looked at his hand, cupped as if holding something but holding nothing.

"Well," he said at last, letting his hand drop. "Remember how everyone was Mister this or Handyman that? I mean, like the UPS guy, or whatever, and Handyman Negri."

123

ODOACER

"Yeah, sure."

"I remember."

Kasey briefly looked to his empty hand again and carried on. "They were working guys, right? And Mr. Rogers was, what?"

"A minister I think."

"I mean on the show. He was just this middle class guy who had them over to his house."

"There was respect!" someone proclaimed.

"It didn't matter who you were," added Chris, looking at his phone. Charles noted that the screen was dark. "You got respect — as an American."

"That was the thing," continued Dan, taking the baton. He half pulled his phone from his pocket, tapped it gently, and slid it back in with a weird smile. "It didn't matter what you did, it was the American dream. Everyone got respect."

Charles added: "if you were white."

The guys stopped, stared at their newest member, adjusted their red hats, and reached for their phones. All looked.

"The king was black," protested Chris.

"Yeah, Chuck, relax. The king was black."

"The king!"

"Yeah, of the land of Make-Believe," someone jested, eliciting a round of guffaws.

"Look," said Chris, taking on his professor role, "The American Dream — it was always there for anyone wanting to take advantage of it, like the King in Mr. Rogers."

"It was always there until it wasn't," said Kasey. "It changed."

"The town changed."

"Look at these families moving into town today," added Kasey. He looked again at his empty hand. "The music."

"Sucks," someone added.

"Thugs," said someone else.

124

ODOACER

"No one calls you mister."

"No one calls you Handyman."

"No one's a handyman."

Dan looked up from his phone. "The king got too big for his britches, if you ask me." He spat out the word king.

They all knew what he meant.

"Wrecked this country!"

"Sold us out!"

BUZZ

All the guys started, even Charles. All looked at their phones, except Kasey, who seemed content to stare at his hand. First there was this one:

> Under my predecessor, America was taken advantage of very badly by NATO, the Japanese and Mexico. Terrible deals. #Betrayed

Then there was this one:

> The world did not respect us. That has changed! Now the world understands that America is not going to get taken advantage of, and things are happening in a major way. Terrific deals on the way. #Respect

And then there was this one:

> Americans are holding their heads high again. All walks of life, it doesn't matter. We are coming together as a nation. #Unity

And finally:

> I am PROCLAIMING May 3 Mr. Rodgers Day in honor of a great American. Kids and adults loved him. Should be required watching still. He shows us the way to a better world.

ODOACER

Kasey was the first to speak. "Goddamn it!" he said, still staring at his hand. "Goddamn it! The fucking guy said it."

"Because he fights for us," someone said.

"We're respected again," cried Dan.

"You know, Obie," Kasey added, "you're right. This place is pretty great."

"This place is great," Scott corrected him.

Kasey exulted, and cried out the President's surname.

Obie and Chris exulted, crying out the President's surname.

Ken, Scott, and Dan, did as well.

And at last Charles Earl Jarlsberg III pumped his fist in the air and proclaimed the familiar monosyllable with what he hoped was sadistic vigor.

Obie's birthday party had, indeed, turned into a proper political event.

CHAPTER TWENTY

THE PRESIDENT'S LATEST TWEETS

It was distracted, yes, distracted. It was distracted from praying. And, in being distracted, it became disconnected. It felt itself falling away from infinity, as though that were possible, into — not infinity.

What was bothering, no, distracting, it, was how mad, how crazy, They had become, how they raged at everything and everyone. How they drove things to crazed ends, to untenable and unpredictable extremes. It was as though They really were — not humors, not a "Them" — but unreflective, purely reactive animal impulses — tinglings in the shoulders, twitches in the lips, involuntary blinkings and scowlings and growlings — somehow personified and made life. That was impossible. There was a plan. The tweets were part of it and They were part of it. And, yet, They wanted to — to *not* follow the plan.

"Get me Freundhein," barked the man that afternoon after digesting the cable news reports in the den of his Florida residence.

No one answered.

ODOACER

"Get me Freundhein," barked the man again, this time into the intercom.

"Yes, Mr. President," replied a voice instantaneously. This was followed, moments later, by a caveat. "He is golfing now, Mr. President. He says he is on his way."

The man fumed. "Tell him not to bother." The intercom clicked off.

The "den" as it was called, was a brightly tiled room, longer than it was wide, with mosaic floors and a bank of slow-rotating ceiling fans along its length. Two sides were comprised of narrow, romanesque arcades, with tinted glass panels, that afforded a view of a palm grove on one side and the links on the other. The furniture was sparse but, by the man's standards, elegant.

The man strolled to a window and glared out of it at the golf course. He had only a narrow view of the action, two holes at the most, and saw no sign of Freundhein. They twitched a bit at this, probably doubting the information that had been provided. But they steadied.

The man removed his phone from his jacket pocket and dialed. It rang, not once, not twice, but thrice before it was answered.

"Boss," came Freundhein's somewhat drawling, somewhat druggy voice. "I'm on my way."

"Forget it Freundhein," said the man. "I'll talk to you now."

There was a pause. A cricket or locust — some bug — chirped or whirred — some sound — in the palm grove. A fly buzzed, thudding futilely, endlessly against the window pane. "Of course, boss. How can I help you?"

"Freundhein, what the fuck are these guys doing?"

"Who?"

"Our friends!" screamed the man. "My friends. The tweets. The — all this." The man gesticulated wildly around the room for no one to see. "All this — this plan."

It noticed.

128

ODOACER

"What seems to be the problem, sir?" said Freudnhein, all business now.

The problem was that tweets sent in the early morning hours had, again, implicated the man in the jewel heist. One in particular said: "Under our PRECIOUS CONSTITUTION, President as commander in chief is solely responsible for national security. Defending national honor demands decisive action." And another: "The Cape Town Emerald was U.S. property that was stolen from America with connivance of crooks in former administration. Jail time?" And: "I will always use the powers of my office as I must to make America great, safe and respected again! #ReturntheEmerald." These tweets had not really been in response to anything. If anything, the jewel heist story had simmered down in the last few days' coverage. If anything, the media narrative had moved on.

Before the tweets, the big story had been the man's off-the-cuff mention, at an official meeting with a foreign dignitary, that he would — not that he would ask his aides to consider, or his commerce department to review, but that he would, personally, reverse course on certain tariffs that were otherwise to have been leveled upon the dignitary's country. Just a day or three earlier, on Twitter, the man had sworn "irrevocably," his word, to impose these tariffs in response to what the man had described as a historically unfair trade relationship that had been negotiated by the usual continuum of clowns and weaklings over decades and nationally humiliating decades.

The new, revised, non-Twitter position had been taken in response to the dignitary's pleas — which were obsequious, self-effacing, and worshipful — which implicitly attributed to the singularity of the man's genius a century of American economic prowess, military dominance, and cultural hegemony — but also it had also been taken on the advice of the Treasury, the Commerce Department, all of the man's economic advisors, most of the crazy billionaire friends with whom he chatted at bedtime, and delegation after delegation of congressional supporters.

ODOACER

The only voice against the backtracking had been Freundhein's, and that had been framed only as a suggestion. "Our friends asked me to let you know that they are awed and inspired by the hard line you've taken with Portugal," he said one time. And, "Our friends wanted me to let you know how impressive it is that you've stood firm on Portugal in the face of Establishment backlash." This last comment was made amidst reports of the aforesaid Congressional delegations.

But Freundhein's had been a lonely voice, and many other more powerful and persuasive advisors had appealed directly to the man's genius, vision, infinite toughness, and unwavering courage on poor Portugal's behalf. And the man had made nice with Portugal.

And that — that story of careful, reasoned reconsideration and international comity — the story of a statesman — was the story for the whole day. Almost.

And then came the tweets.

"I see what you're saying, sir," said Freundhein, over the phone, when all had been explained to him. "I think, perhaps, the idea is that America wants to see you as the strong, decisive leader that you are, and perhaps our friends want to make clear that you will stop at nothing." He paused, evidently fishing for words. "At no legal or constitutional barrier," he continued, with just a hint of menace, "in your fight on behalf of the American people."

The man said nothing. The man's shoulders, however, slumped a bit, along with his humongous head. The man looked at his shoes, straightened his tie. It could feel them, just barely: aching, resentful, but subdued.

"Okay, Freundhein," said the man at long last. "I see. Just?"

"Yes, sir?"

"Freundhein," the man's voice cracked. "Tell them just to let me — this one time. It's not a very big thing. Portugal."

The good doctor said nothing for a moment. He was no doubt nodding, in his sad way, into the phone.

130

ODOACER

"No, sir. I suppose it's not a very big thing."

"Just this one time?"

"I'll ask, Mr. President."

CHAPTER TWENTY-ONE

HOT WAR

After the unpleasant exchange in the trophy room, former senior presidential advisor Peter S. Donovan avoided discussions of politics and quickly — if somewhat artificially — Mona's captivity at Trois-Fois-Maître returned to its usual rhythms. The banging continued, as unsatisfying as ever but by now a matter of habit, as did the tittering at *mots*, and the meals and after-dinner aperitifs in the trophy room. For the last week or more, nearly every conversation at these events had circled back to the theme of Eastern mysticism — a subject in relation to which Donovan and von Stilicho battled to outdo one another in sheer pretentiousness. At last it had been determined that, between Donovan's world-historic perspective and the Chevalier's evidently copious "field work," they could profitably collaborate on an article despite any differences of opinion — and with surprising persistence they resumed "brainstorming" each time they'd achieved a suitable level of drunkenness.

The new element in the routine was what Mona came to regard as her spelunking expeditions into the castle's bowels. Each night after completing the simple feat of wearing out von

ODOACER

Stilicho, she'd sneak down to the trophy room, molest Atreus, and return to her perch.

Donovan's ritual, though occurring at odd and irregular hours, followed a fairly standard script. He'd watch his monitors — particularly when certain Hammer News shows were on — until he found inspiration in some bit of frustration, rage, or off-the-cuff observation, then he'd translate what he'd heard into the President's familiar cadences and post. He'd afterward watch, with evident mirth, the reaction of whoever inspired the tweet, and thereby confirm the strengthening of sentimental bonds between Leader and Led.

Roughly speaking, Donovan had four tricks. The first and most frequently observed was the simple feedback loop: the official regurgitating of public sentiment, the more authentically irrational the better. This wildly successful enterprise, apparently, was the great engine of national rebirth.

The second trick was what Mona had observed with the son's appointment and the Portuguese poultry tariffs: arbitrary and disruptive policy pronouncements that served no broader goal, but exploded in the faces of bureaucrats and experts, the retired of whom responded in flurries of on-air hand-wringing. It wasn't really policy but anti-policy — contempt for the very idea of policy that, Mona intuited, was part and parcel of Donovan's famous contempt for state institutions. And the President, who of course meant what he said and said what he meant, never, ever, ever backed down from these positions, once taken, forcing his now firmly anti-policy policy apparatus to commit the machinery of state to whatever Peter S. Donovan had made the President tweet on Twitter. That was one and two.

Three and four were of a slightly different character. Three was what Mona called the goading: committing the President to a really bad and self-destructive course of action in one way or another. So it was that one night Donovan tweeted comments in the context of a hush money scandal that, though denying the President's participation in the alleged fucking and cover-up, did little for the dignity of the office and, more to the point, had the natural and predictable effect of prompting the President to double down on the denials in terms that would likely waive whatever attorney-client privileged once attached to his interactions with a now wavering personal fixer. The weeks of boasts and threats preceding the President's retention of von Stilicho — although Mona hadn't observed their creation — surely fit into this category. Donovan had simply made things such that a man of the President's character couldn't look at himself in the mirror if he *didn't* steal the Cape Town Sapphire. And that brought Mona to the fourth kind of tweet:

Threats and chastisement. These were the tweets in which Donovan had the President obliquely confess to something, or otherwise expose him to immediate, public trouble. So it was that, every third night or so, the President would revisit the saga of the Cape Town Emerald, as he called it, usually in a manner that both revived the sagging scandal and suggested, without out-right admitting, that the President had stolen the gem and was proud of the fact he had.

Thus number three worked with number four: with one Tweet, Donovan would goad the President into larceny, and with the next he'd threaten, in his way, to give up the store. So he controlled the man, or imagined that he did, and through him carried out the important work — his life's work — performed by Tweet tricks one and two: the forging of the nation and the obliteration of the state.

"I think that's the whole story," she told the Chevalier quietly while they were both under the blanket. "That's what he's up to."

He looked up from what he was doing and wiped his lips with the back of his wrist. "What happens, I wonder, when the President discovers that the Nation doesn't care about a stolen gemstone anymore?"

Mona frowned. "You can't just stop in the middle like that, von Stilicho."

"Apologies," he said, resuming his post.

ODOACER

But von Stilicho was right. It was but a matter of time.

And time passed. One evening in mid-May, Mona arrived late to dinner to find Donovan silently sipping from a flask. The Chevalier, who'd taken his seat, began a couple pointless anecdotes about ashrams and zen gardens before falling silent under his host's grim stare.

"Ah, Ms. France," Donovan said at last, his pallid, splotchy complexion clashing with the glittery baby-blue, ankle-length (with a train) muumuu he'd put on for the evening. "I apologize for the imposition. You must find our all our talk of oriental spirituality very dull."

Mona smiled weakly and shrugged her shoulders, unsure whether Donovan meant to offend von Stilicho with the word "dull" or herself with the term "oriental." She did not intend to be goaded again.

"Ah! Is Pete a bit testy today?" jested von Stilicho to a stony response.

"Please, Mr. Donovan," added Mona. "It's been so pleasant since — "

The husky former presidential advisor fixed a mean stare on her. "Since what, Ms. France? Since we discussed politics."

Mona frowned. "There are some things — I think — Mr. Donovan — that are better left alone. Now, come, I thought the Chevalier said something interesting about sufism the other day. What was that, von Stilicho?"

"Yes, you see, it was during my sojourn in the Takla Makan. I had taken up with —"

Donovan waved a hand dismissively and took another swig from his flask as a Proud-boy loped in with a tray of bland-looking sandwich wraps. These were not up to Donovan's usual epicurean standards and suggested a certain distractedness on the part of the kitchen staff and, behind them, their lord and master.

Von Stilicho nonetheless dug into a tuna wrap with abandon.

ODOACER

"I get it, Ms. France," growled Donovan. "You'd rather pretend things are —"

"Are what, Mr. Donovan?" she snapped.

"Are different from what they are."

Here they come, thought Mona with a shudder. The hard truths. Here, if allowed, Donovan will tell her some unpleasant fact about race relations in America and the factors of biological determinism that underpin them. Then he would almost certainly circle back to the harmonious and sentimentally unified whole that is his incipient Nation of shirtless stevedores and hitchhikers. She would not let him.

"Yes, Mr. Donovan. Frankly, I'd rather pretend. And perhaps if we pretend long enough, we'll make the world so. That seems to be your premise, anyhow. And I shall make it mine. Now, would you pass me a roast beef, please?"

Donovan guffawed darkly and did as he was asked. Taking another sip, he added, "Very well, Ms. France, von Stilicho. In that case, I shall excuse myself."

The Lord of Trois-Fois-Maître thereupon rose and left, Proud-boys at his side, as Mona dejectedly attacked her roast beef wrap and the Chevalier — as though nothing had happened or was happening — basked happily in the evening sun.

"Very well, dear," he said. "Shall we repair to our apartments? I must say I'm rather in the mood to —"

Mona shushed him. "Not now, von Stilicho," she said. "I want to see what he's up to." And with that thought Mona France upped and left supper, destination: the tunnels.

She knew she shouldn't be doing this in daylight, while the household staff was up and about. But she needed to know the reason for Donovan's dark mood, what it heralded for their continuing captivity, and for the fate of both nations — the one of law and the other of the never-ending feedback loop. So in she went, silently, speedily, to her perch behind the control room. And there he found Donovan hard at work.

He was ensconced in his throne, staring somewhat blankly as the large monitor, upon which was a test pattern

ODOACER

counting down to zero. When it had, after a short burst of static, there appeared on the screen the vaguely familiar appearance of Dr. Todd Freundhein, M.D., personal physician to the President of the United States of America. He was as always grizzled, almost avuncular with his disheveled hair and beard. If only to remind the world that he was a doctor, he wore a white lab coat and a polished head mirror on a leather strap.

"Donovan," he said with a slight smile.

"Freundhein," came the hoarse response.

"I am prepared to make my report."

Donovan raised his hand. "That is not necessary, Freundhein."

The good doctor made a look that was vaguely stunned and hurt, but not excessively so, then continued: "Then how may I be of assistance?"

"Doctor," replied Donovan, "I am concerned that we are losing our grip on this — situation."

"How so, Donovan?"

"Portugal."

Confusion flashed across Freundhein's brow, followed in due course by a kind of half-witted enlightenment. "Oh that," he said. "It is not a serious —"

"Freundhein!" barked Donovan. "We cannot have an asset overruling our considered judgments."

The doctor paused for a moment, evidently gathering his thoughts. "But how does it even matter? Tariffs on Portugal?"

"It matters," Donovan replied firmly, "because we said there were going to be tariffs on Portuguese —" His speech trailed off.

"Chickens, I think," offered Dr. Freundhein.

"Yes, chickens, whatever. We said it and, what happens next?"

"You must understand, Donovan. You're not here. I mean, the pressures are tremendous. Senators, Congressmen, all the experts and — even the business guys on Hammer —"

"That," interrupted Donovan, shouting now, "is precisely the point. Fuck those guys, Freundhein. Fuck all of them. That's exactly the kind of shit we're against."

It was almost shocking to hear Donovan speak like that. Oh, of course, before being kidnapped by him, Mona had always expected he'd talk like this: fuck these people, we're against that shit. But his speech during their captivity had been, on the whole, modulated and, with the exceptions, polite, even dreamy. Now he was speaking like a hard-nosed political operative.

Specifically, like a hard-nosed political operative whose life's work was about to go sideways in a truly catastrophic manner.

"This is policy bullshit," Donovan continued. "This is government by a bunch of fucking eggheads and the the fucking chamber of commerce. We're supposed to smash this crap, Freundhein. That's why we're in this game."

Freundhein stroked his beard. "But this is a minor —
"

"No, Freundhein!" Donovan brought a fist down on the armrest. "There are no minor things. Every emanation of the popular will is equal to the next. It's what you call the minor stuff that's, if anything, most important. Because that's what the frigging elites think can be safely ignored as irrational bullshit from the rubes."

"We can't accomplish everything."

Donovan screamed in response: "THERE. IS. ONLY. ONE. THING. FREUNDHEIN."

The doctor flinched, mouth agape, and said nothing as he waited for Donovan's heated, heavy breathing to subside.

This took all of a minute.

"Dr. Freundhein," the Lord of Trois-Fois-Maître said at last, "I am going to unleash hell. When it happens, he will come to you." Donovan paused, stroked his chin. It wasn't obvious that this was a wholly thought-out plan. But it was evidently an emanation of the popular will and not to be ignored, particularly by some prick with a medical degree.

ODOACER

"Make sure, when he does, Freundhein, that he knows why this is happening."

"Yes, Pete. Yes, I understand." This was the sad, low-energy response.

Donovan banged on the armrest console and the screen went blank. He spun around two or three times in his throne, then leaned over and made a series of swishing noises that attracted a large Siamese cat. This Donovan took into his arms and stroked gently.

Once more, his shoulders straightened. He gently set the cat on the floor and adjusted a knob on his control panel. The small, bulbous monitors popped to life: all those bars and diners and barber shops and church basements. Donovan had the sound on toggle, so it flipped from one to the next.

The President's open Twitter account was now transferred from one of the side monitors to the large main one directly in front of the former senior presidential advisor. He thereupon began typing. Mona watched the characters dance across the screen: after a few revisions and deletions, these had arranged themselves into the following words:

"The Cape Emeralds are beautiful American national hairlooms . . ."

That word was in fact spelled "hairlooms."

"As President I had COMPLETE AUTHORITY to protect the homeland and its terrific heritage. And I DID IT!"

Then Donovan hit post, and the tweet was posted.

On one of the monitors, a man in a barbershop glanced at his phone and then said to his barber: "'bout time he said that."

"Sure is," said the barber. "Now hold still."

The sound toggled to another monitor — the church basement this time.

"Yes, please!" exclaimed a man wearing a polo shirt tucked into khaki slacks. "Yes, just let's move on."

"Don't even see why this is a thing," said the man next to him, who was twenty years older, a father-in-law perhaps, and wore a vinyl jacket.

139

ODOACER

The next tweet said: "Dishonest media criticizes my beautiful hotel in DC. It's the best place in town. Of course foreign dignitaries want to stay there. They should! And I'm always happy to talk with our friends who enjoy luxury." This was sent.

"See if they like hearing that you're a crook," Donovan exulted.

They did. It suited them just fine.

"Makes sense," said a fat man at a diner, showing his phone to his waitress.

"Honey, I know how the world works," she said. "Let the man do what he's got to."

"It's a beautiful hotel," said her companion who, passing by on her way to the kitchen caught the gist of her comments. "Saw it when we went there."

Donovan flinched and got back to work.

Another: "Hypocritical news media pries into my personal life in order to devastate my family. They're going strong! Media wants to distract from winning record on immigration & economy. American people don't care who I've been with, just what I'm accomplishing."

This was sent. Mona shuttered.

"You're in hot water now," grumbled Pete Donovan.

But he — the President — wasn't. He wasn't at all.

Another diner, but the people were essentially the same. A woman in a Christian camp T-shirt said, after reading the tweet, "Yeah, so what if he gets around?"

To which a man in a flannel shirt, tucked in, with suspenders framing his overhanging gut, replied: "What a dog!"

The woman said back to him, "Right? Men will be men."

Donovan set aside the keyboard and stared in astonishment at all the little gray, really white, people flitting across the monitors. The same thing was happening, everywhere, more or less the same way.

ODOACER

"I'm glad he stole that diamond," droned a fat woman somewhere.

"If I could make a buck off a hotel, I would too," twanged a skinny man.

"Who wouldn't screw a playmate!" exulted a young executive.

And so on.

Fat woman: "He stole it *for us*."

Skinny man: "It's *our* hotel." The young executive grabbed three kleenex and a bottle of hand lotion and, happily, wandered off camera.

"Fine!" Donovan yelled at no one and nothing. He was breathing harder than Mona had seen him breathe. He slumped, gathered himself, and then typed.

"Media drives false narrative about collusion. No collusion! I am increasing sanctions on Russia to unpresidented levels and plan to implement joint navel exercises in the Baltic with our good friends Finland and Sweden."

This he sent.

The message registered on the little monitors, but without an excess of excitement.

"Yeah, you show'm" muttered a man at a bar before ordering himself a drink.

"Shows what a bullshit hoax this is, this Russia thing," said his drinking buddy, mostly to himself.

And in a living room somewhere, a man said in honest disbelief to his doughy wife, "Don't even see why they're supposed to be our enemies — jus' want what we want."

"Mm-hmm."

With a flick of a switch on his armrest, the former presidential advisor muted the ever-toggling sound feed from the little monitors. With the flick of another, he brought an image up on his big monitor, the one which, up to now, he'd been composing the President's tweets and almost-tweets.

The image appeared to be coming from the camera on a computer somewhere. It was a wide shot of a big, high-

ODOACER

ceilinged room festooned with all manner of rococo fixtures and gold woodwork. The walls bore portraits of proud-looking men — on horseback, haranguing crowds, staring off at horizons, in some cases merely sitting for official portraits.

In front of all these, seated at a desk, directly in front of the computer: a man, small, colorless, with thinning hair, a thin mustache and a cheap suit. He was scribbling out words on the page of a notebook, ignoring the computer.

An off-camera voice called out and the man's attention was diverted to its source. It was speaking in a language Mona didn't know. All she could make out, again and again, was the name "Odoacer" and the word "tweet."

The man at the desk nodded, dismissed his informant with a curt wave, and leveled his gaze at the camera, which is to say his computer screen. There was the click of a mouse, another, and then the man's eyes moved back and forth, once, twice, thrice. Rereading the words on his screen — that was certainly what he was doing — he brought a fist down on his desk. He started shouting something in the same language. Mona didn't know for sure, but this very probably translated to:

"Who the fuck does this guy think he is?"

Donovan shut off the sound, diminished the feed, and leaned back. He signed, then let out a dry, ill-humored chuckle.

"Beat that," he muttered.

Tucked away in her hidey-hole, unseen, Mona France was certain of exactly one thing. She was certain that the President would beat that.

CHAPTER TWENTY-TWO

EZIO'S TRUE ECONOMIC INTERESTS

Charles strode up the steps to Ezio's front porch, a sagging affair, long ago walled-in to create a damp and cavernous anteroom that was now cluttered, to boot, with magazines, a disorganized pile of tools, and discarded cardboard boxes. He knocked twice as he crossed the threshold and, with the familiarity of an old friend, approached the door to the house proper.

"It's open," Ezio called out from somewhere inside the house. "That you, Charles?"

"Yes, Ezio." Charles entered his comrade's home. It was dark, carpeted wall to wall, wood-paneled. A TV was on but no one was watching it.

"I'm in the back," said Ezio. "In Beeb's room."

Beeb was Ezio's young son, whom he raised with the help of Thekla's mother and sister. Beeb — a portmanteau of initials, the significance of which Charles hadn't bothered to learn — suffered from a chronic medical condition that, although eminently treatable, was incurable, uncomfortable, and, for his care-givers, a source of constant worry.

143

ODOACER

Charles tossed a six pack of beer into the fridge. "I brought beer," he said. There wasn't much else in it: a ginger ale bottle, a carton from a Chinese restaurant, stained through with grease at the bottom, a few sad looking vegetables, some cheese. The freezer, which surely was well stocked with frozen entrees and ice cream, would be where the action was.

"Thanks," said Ezio.

Charles opened a beer, took a sip, and smiled with a nervous anticipation of what must come next.

Earlier in the day the President of the United States, having campaigned on the promise of replacing his predecessor's health insurance initiative with a cheaper but vastly more expansive system, had, after a string of legislative failures, instructed his Secretary of Health and Human Services — in the course of a meandering address to the Education Department, no less — to issue certain waivers to states, and to withhold certain funds, in such manner as to invite the outcome that fewer people would be covered by the program at any one time, and that those who were covered would have to pay significantly higher premiums. That is, after the President had suggested to his congressional allies that the socialistic status quo should be replaced by "universal medicare," he had simply surrendered to the ideologues in the party establishment and set about sabotaging any recent advances.

This, Charles figured, coupled with the Beeb's troubled condition, might create the necessary material conditions for Ezio's awakening to true consciousness and, of course, His True Interests.

Charles found Ezio huddled over Beeb's bed. The child was evidently having one of his "bouts," which made him spacey and cranky, and occasionally violent. Charles daubed his forehead tenderly with a wadded up cloth in which he'd wrapped a handful of ice cubes. The room was dark, save for the glow of a little desk lamp, and, with his free hand, Ezio read to the boy from a Dr. Seuss book.

ODOACER

"I am sorry," Charles said as he entered. "I — shouldn't intrude."

"No, no," said Ezio with a sad smile. "No, I'm glad for the company. Sit down." He gestured to an old wicker chair piled high with books. "He's almost asleep. Or, better yet, go watch TV. I'll be out in a minute."

Charles did as instructed. It was almost half an hour before Ezio had finished tending to the boy. Once he did, he grabbed a beer himself and sat down in the easy chair beside Charles'.

"O, god damn, I can't watch this today," he said, nodding toward Patrick O'Rourke's pill-shaped head ranting on Hammer News. Charles changed the channel.

After Ezio had taken a swig of his beer, and then another, Charles spoke up. "So," he said, "did you hear the news today?"

"No, what? Oh!" Ezio smiled. "That. Sure did."

Charles nodded gravely.

"How will you care for Beeb?"

"What?"

"Will you be able to care for Beeb?"

"Sure. I always do." He took another pull of his beer can. "I thought you wanted to talk about the news."

"Yes." Charles grimaced.

Ezio stared fleetingly at his palm and chuckled. "I'm glad as hell he took that fucking thing, you know."

"What thing?"

"The ruby or whatever."

"Yes," said Charles, remembering who he was supposed to be. He flashed what he hoped to be a convincing smile and toasted the air with his beer can. "Yes, pretty great."

Charles grabbed himself another beer, along with one for his friend, and fixated on the television. Something about nazi construction projects. It leaned heavily on jarring, Wagnerian, notes of music, and on nazi newsreels filmed from theatrical angles — the stirring effects of which it rather lamely

145

balanced out with the narrated reminders that the masterminds of these impressive projects were "evil" and "sick."

Charles would try again.

"But Ezio," he said during the commercial break. "These guys in Congress, you know. They're elites. They're not for us. They're for Andrew. This thing with the waivers or whatever — that's what they want, but. How will you take care of Beeb if?"

Ezio sipped his beer and stared intently at his outstretched, open hand. He smiled, gave a chuckle of relief, and, upon another moment reflection, shrugged his shoulder philosophically. "Ah. I'll figure something out."

Then he chuckled again.

"And with the hotel? I mean, damn straight. Make hay while the sun shines." He was again staring at his palm. God that must have pissed fucking Andrew off. Am I right?"

That night, over beers, Charles hit on a new idea. Perhaps Ezio would not ever come to understand what Charles understood to be His True Interests — or, at any rate, to rank them above the interests that so thrilled at the prospect of "owning" Andrew or sticking it to the Mexicans. But perhaps, nevertheless, he could have other interests. Interests undeniable and irreconcilable with the President's agenda.

And, most of all, he wanted to.

So — and this needn't be detailed at length — after a few more drinks — Charles had to make a "run" — Charles made an overture which was not rebuffed. Both found it satisfying and, upon waking up, agreed it was weird but, that, between the two of them, perhaps they should be an "item."

But Ezio would feel more comfortable, and Charles couldn't object, if they maybe waited a while before breaking it to the rest of the guys.

CHAPTER TWENTY-THREE

OUT OF CONTROL

Much as it was in community with the infinite, much as it professed indifference to the contingent, it was nevertheless taken aback by the barrage of tweets — all attributed to the man — that had landed in the late night hours. These were all highly embarrassing to the operation. Whoever was writing them — the anonymous friends who spoke only to good Freundhein — heretofore proponents of the operation — was sending Them a warning. But the latest was needlessly provocative and presaged a break, potentially a fatal break.

It blamed the friends, it blamed Them. Was it alone innocent and pure?

The tweets had hit a couple days earlier, and since then it, the man, They, the whole operation had been lying low.

One tweet had effectively admitted, on the man's behalf, to stealing the Cape Town Sapphire, even boasted about it. A second openly invited bribes, to the man, from foreign governments. The next had admitted to an extramarital affair by the man. And the fourth and weirdest had challenged Russia in the Baltic, prompting that erstwhile benefactor to threaten all manner of retaliation if molested on

ODOACER

that sea and, worse, to drop a morsel about some stupid thing in Baku it only vaguely remembered.

How long could this go on?

It was waiting for the hammer to drop. It was waiting for the Congressional loyalists to waiver, for friendly pundits and talking heads to say — enough! — it was waiting for Hammer to drop its endless defenses. It was waiting for the man's public to abandon him.

They were waiting too. They raged.

"Freundhein!" went the man, barking into an intercom. "Get me Freundhein."

"Right away, Mr. President," came the response.

The fingers danced across the smooth surface of the phone.

Responses on Twitter were — from the fans, anyhow — resoundingly positive.

The headlines on all the usual sites were — positive. Supportive.

A hand flicked on the TV. A talking head was talking to solemnly nodding, but not talking, heads: ". . . the President tells it like it is . . ."

Flip to the liberal channel: ". . . this President communicates directly with his base . . ."

And to the "fair" channel: ". . . well, this is really how ordinary people talk. And they expect forcefulness from their leaders. And I think that resonates with voters . . ."

Into the desk phone, the man spoke: "Get me Carl. Now." The man continued flipping through the channels, surfing over the internet, returning to chatrooms and twitter feeds. It was all — ordinary. His congressional loyalists were loyal. The friendly pundits and talking heads were friendly. Hammer was Hammer.

It watched all of this with what it assured itself was its usual detachment, but couldn't help being intrigued by it.

"Yes, Mr. President?" Carl's voice.

It could feel Them — their gears clicking and whirring. The heat of rage had subsided into something exultant. The full power of Their will was rushing past like a river, rushing toward some definite point. A plan. They were devising a masterstroke. It was sure of this.

"Carl. What's the latest polling? Since the tweets?"

"It's a bit early to know, sir."

"It doesn't need to be perfect," was the barked response. "Get me anything. A daily, a snap poll. Get me whatever's out there."

"Yes, Mr. President. I'll call—"

"No, I'll wait."

A knock came on the door. The man cradled the receiver between head and shoulder. "Come in," he said hoarsely, with a wave no-one could see.

Freundhein entered. He was smiling — but he was smiling nervously. The man smiled menacingly at his doctor. It was the kind of smile the man gave someone he knew was trying to rip him off. It was the only sincere smile the man ever gave. And, as Freundhein melted before him, the smile settled into a furious scowl. The scowl of the official portraits. "Sit down, Freundhein. I'm on the phone."

The doctor seated himself in a divan chair by the door, upholstered in gold cloth partly eaten through. He did not try to meet the man's gaze, but instead stared at his feet, which swung like a child's, back and forth, over the side of the chair. He was wearing sneakers.

"Mr. President?"

"Yes, Carl. What do we have?"

"Just dailies, one snap polls. Nothing I'd call statistically meaningful."

"And?"

"No real movement in popularity or approval. Maybe a little boost — two or three points — among supporters. I got one snap poll of registered party members — our party — about the tweets."

"And?"

"Well, it's not a significant sampling, but —"

"Just tell me."

149

ODOACER

"A couple people said they wish you'd tweet less, sir. But no one — or hardly anyone — said he'd less likely support you as a result. And, uh, among strong supporters, they're agreeing with phrases like, uh, 'telling it like it is,' 'refreshing,' and, um, here, 'brave.'"

The man said nothing. The breathing was heavy, steady, focused — it was a raging bull's breath. It must have terrified Carl.

The man looked to Freundhein. And again the man smiled. It wasn't an angry or suspicious smile this time. It was the contented smile of a hunter who had cornered his prey. The only other sincere smile the man ever gave.

"Thanks, Carl." The man hung up the phone.

The man stepped toward Freundhein. "And now, Freundhein?"

The doctor looked up. He was terrified.

"Now you're going to tell me who they are and where they are."

The man's enormous shadow enveloped the cowering doctor. Freundhein's jaw hung loose, his lips quivered.

"Now, Freundhein."

The scene that followed with Freundhein was distressing. He broke immediately. There wasn't even a fight. The man needed only let it be know that he was asserting his independence. It was given without formalities. The doctor slumped back in the divan and sobbed softly, mumbling incoherent nonsense about mistakes made and regrets.

The man slapped him.

Freundhein looked up at the man with almost complete indifference. His eyes and cheeks were red, and wet from tears, his hair disheveled, his mouth agape. It was the look of a person who had already surrendered to whatever fate had in store, as though nothing could be gained or lost by any course of action, and all that remained to be done whatever the man asked of him.

Freundhein told the man everything. In soft, matter-of-fact sentences, interspersed with effusions of quiet sobs, he told all:

That Donovan controlled the Twitter account.

That Donovan was ensconced at a fortified installation in a town on the northern Californian coast.

That the town was called Tercero Maestro.

That the installation was guarded by a small army of telepathically controlled servants.

That Donovan possessed certain compromising information on the man, including, without limitation, that the man had ordered the theft of the Cape Town Sapphire — Emerald, sorry — and, through an eminently traceable network of small-time lawyers and Delaware LLCs, was in possession of assorted photos, documents and receipts that might be embarrassing to a lesser man.

That Donovan had in his custody two persons — a girl lawyer called Mona something and the Chevalier Ritter von Stilicho — who also possessed much of this information and were threatening to use it against the man.

That the Chevalier Ritter von Stilicho was strongly suspected of being the famed cat burglar, Le Chien, and may possess first-hand knowledge of the man's involvement in the heist, as well as documentary evidence of the same.

That Donovan would — if provoked — destroy the man by releasing this information.

That Donovan would — if provoked — destroy the man by making him out to be a madman via the twitter account.

At this, the man had laughed. It was the first time the man had laughed in many, many years. It was a simple, loud, "Ha!" that reverberated through the building.

The man had grabbed Freundhein by the lapels and lifted. He might not have been up to the effort — the man did not exercise — but Freundhein meekly stood. "Does that fat shit really think anyone cares about that? About any of that?"

The man tossed Freundhein into the corner of the room, where he collapsed without protest. The man, towering over his limp form, gave the good doctor a swift kick in the ribs.

"No one cares, Freundhein. Did you know that? If anything, I'm up. I just heard as much from Carl."

The man kicked the doctor again.

"So, Donovan has nothing on me. Nothing. There's nothing he can do to me."

The man had stood back and rubbed the hands together. The man smiled.

"But there's plenty I can do to him, Freundhein. Plenty."

After that, events had passed in a whirlwind. It could hardly even follow them. But it experienced — at first mildly, but all the more acutely as things developed, a sense of, not so much unease, not so much fear or frustration, but of resentment.

What were They doing? What was Their game?

Oh, it knew that They had important roles to play. That neither the man nor the operation was a self-sustaining gift. There was work to do, and it had been content with Their execution of Their tasks.

But!

They would be free. They would take control — complete control — of the plan, which had now surpassed Freundhein and Donovan. They would stand in complete, unmediated communion with Their public. And, once they did, the power — the man's power, but America's power too — would be all but unlimited.

It heard a voice in all this that, it knew, was its own voice, and it said: what about me?

What about me?

Well, what about me? It started at this thought. At the use of this word. What, and who, was it even talking about? Who was me?

ODOACER

It prayed for guidance on this, and found none. No one and nothing answered.

Meanwhile, in the world, things went on.

The man had Freundhein tossed in the White House brig, then called his chief of staff. Military advisors were called in and consulted. Plans were made. Security forces, investigative and enforcement wings of various agencies were mobilized. As a perhaps unnecessary formality, warrants were even sought and quickly granted.

Meanwhile, the man had let it be known that he wished to address the nation. Not on twitter, but on the television. All channels, primetime — it would be a ratings bonanza. Because, actually, he had to deliver his most important message ever.

In the interval between this announcement and the 8 o'clock address, the twitter account exploded, but it was like no one was paying attention anymore. It became only noise. It was the inner workings of a mind — a private matter. The things thought, but not said aloud — no man could be faulted for that. We have freedom of conscience in this country, after all. The President's conscience too.

It was alone. It was abandoned. What about me? What about me?

The address began at eight, but the man kept the nation waiting until 8:10. Then the nation saw the man sitting at his desk, hands clasped, scowling. His eyes looked dead ahead, like he was condemning the viewer in his home. He was not using a teleprompter. The words rolled out from his mouth. The address was brief.

"My fellow Americans," he said. "The last decade has been a time of unprecedented polarization in the country."

That would win the man plaudits on cable TV for offering an olive branch, for striving for a bipartisan tone.

"I wish to end this polarization. That is why I'm calling for all Americans, regardless of their political affiliations or beliefs, to participate in Restore America rallies this Saturday at 12 noon. Events will be organized in all major cities and

ODOACER

most towns. But I personally will be at the event in San Francisco, California."

"These events will be patriotic, non-partisan opportunities to celebrate the accomplishments of this administration, including an economy that is growing without any precedent in modern history, and the appointment of a Supreme Court justice. It's really, really terrific.

"My friends, I am calling for the end of partisanship as we know it. We should, instead of fighting each other as partisans, reflect upon, and celebrate, the great things we have done together as a nation since I took office nearly two years ago.

"Accordingly, I have chosen to address the event in San Francisco. It's going to be huge. Maybe the biggest ever. I have chose this city because, in the name of burying the hatchet on partisanship, I thought it was important that I show myself as a friend in enemy territory. And this I am — a friend.

"I think you should all go. I promise it will be great."

The man smiled.

"And I think there are going to be some fireworks."

The address had ended.

The cameras shut off. A gaggle of security and advance men, policy makers and press people mobbed the man seeking guidance for planning the just-announced event. They were told to make it happen — but a few of the generals were directed to attend a meeting later that evening in the parlour off the man's bedroom. Some special, technical planning was needed.

Then the man had gone to his room. The last night's pajamas lay on the floor, where the man left them. A damp towel was draped over the back of an old armchair, where the man had draped it. The sock drawer was open. The household staff had, as instructed, not entered. The man was in control.

He strode to the bathroom. The man's eyes were directed at the mirror.

ODOACER

It took a look. It takes a look.

Yes, the man was older than he'd been, puffier, oranger, somewhat more ridiculous looking. The man entered scowling, but that soon turned to mere frowning, and then to smiling, and, it thought, in a way, yes, the man still looked handsome. He wore suit and tie, even in private, didn't even loosen the tie or unbutton the shirt. It was not a well-fitting suit, but that wasn't important. It was expensive, and if it signaled a certain contempt for convention, that was no doubt just what They were aiming for.

The man just stood there smiling. The man's teeth gleamed. He was a winner.

They were winning. So much winning.

What about me? it thought.

What about me? thought the man.

And, just for a fraction of a moment, the man's lip twitched, the man's eyes became unfocused and afraid.

The man winced.

CHAPTER TWENTY-FOUR

A FAILURE OF NERVE

The mood in Chateau Trois-Fois-Maître had darkened considerably over recent days. Tittering at *mots* had all but ceased, save to the extent von Stilicho tittered at his own. Donovan seldom showed up for meals and, when he did, he would already be well into a flask. He growled and grumbled, pointedly avoided talk of Eastern mysticism and even the Civil War, and made peevish, passive aggressive remarks about Mona's steadfast refusal to discuss politics with him. "Someday it'll matter who stood up to be counted at this moment," he'd grumble, an angry stare fixed on the young attorney. Two days earlier he'd started making grim jests about the "bigoted uncle at Thanksgiving dinner" — a persona he presumably adopted for himself — and asked Mona how she'd handle herself in that situation.

"I get the joke, Mr. Donovan," she'd said. "I don't have a racist uncle, or bigoted uncle. But I'm familiar with the metaphor."

"And you accept its premise?"

"That people get in arguments with racist uncles at Thanksgiving? Sure, I guess."

156

ODOACER

"No — that that argument is a metaphor for our national debate."

Mona had shaken her head, exasperated. "I don't know, Mr. Donovan. Sure. It doesn't matter."

Donovan had smiled weakly at this concession — his first substantive triumph in weeks — and, jabbing an accusatory index finger in Mona's direction, snickered: "But you see, this metaphor — which you liberal humanists love — " Mona hated the metaphor and hadn't been accused of liberal humanism in some time. Ever, in fact. "In it, you understand, there's an acceptance of who's doing the debating and what's being debated. You see? There's an implicit acceptance of what the political system does and doesn't embrace."

"I told you I'm not debating you, Mr. Donovan," was Mona's firm response. And with that, the husky former senior presidential advisor had deflated. He had excused himself from the table a few face-saving moments later.

Mona understood, of course, why the Lord of Trois-Fois-Maître was down in the dumps. He'd played almost his entire hand, and his hand was a bust.

The news shows had for almost six hours treated the apparent admission of sapphire theft — or, as they all dutifully reported it now, emerald theft — as a genuine earth-shaking revelation. But the President's Congressional defenders and media flacks had all stayed on message: This was old news (it was), the President was fighting for the American people, and the American people wanted to move on from this issue which, first of all, was now fully resolved and, second, had grown awfully boring.

The sexual escapades and emolument racketeering likewise made no headway. A narrative quickly and successfully took hold: this was all the way of the world, and of powerful men in particular, and what was different here was that it was all out in the open. And thus the President, for deceiving the public so shoddily, was awarded points for honesty.

157

ODOACER

The Russians, for their part, had responded to Donovan's provocation with bellicosity, but little in the way of revelation. Whatever they had on the President, all they let slip in this instance was a tidbit about a suspicious — if only because previously undisclosed — 2013 meeting in Baku between a second-tier oligarch and some one or more of the President's spawn. The subject of the meeting, a subsequently aborted negotiation over a branded resort outside that city that nonetheless seemed to have resulted in several tens of millions of dollars being shifted around foreign bank accounts, hardly rated mention on the evening news.

"Of course, the Russians may have more," Mona has whispered to the Chevalier after watching said evening news on the TV set in the billiard room.

"I suppose so, my love." He yawned. "But having the goods on a President is worth a lot more to them than having given up the goods on an ex-President."

"Yes, I thought of that von Stilicho. Now please try to concentrate on what you're doing, because —"

But von Stilicho had fallen asleep.

Donovan's sessions in the control room — which Mona had continued to observe — had in the meantime become both more listless and more desperate. He would go hours and hours, sometimes, without so much as a tweet. He just stared at the little screens in seeming disbelief as the little gray people reacted their ways through their lives. There was, increasingly, a harmony to their sentiments: as though each was anticipating and verbalizing the frustration or rage of the next. One day they'd all be going off on Central Americans, the next day it would be football protesters, and the day after that it would be the incivility of their political foes. It was no longer clear, really, where it was coming from. Sometimes the popular sentiment displayed on the little screens followed a pronouncement by the President or a segment on Hammer news. But just as often, now, the sentiment preceded these things.

ODOACER

Everyone, Mona recognized with a shiver, was on the same page. Everyone except Donovan, that is. He had made his nation and lost it too.

The irony was not lost on him. He's watch the little screens and mutter, "All's lost, all's lost," and then, "but it's done, yes it's happening," and, "it has outgrown me," the last said with a little chuckle, to be followed by the most unmanly sobs.

And then, to make matters even worse, he had lost contact with Freundhein. Through the initial stages of the crisis, the arch-manipulator and the handler had been in nearly daily contact. The doctor had reported, with increasing nervousness, that President was buoyed by positive polling, unconcerned by the public confessions, and, more and more, furious at him, good Doc Freundhein, and, moreover, at the Friends, whoever they were, that had been running the operation.

"But I think," the doctor had said hopefully, "when this thing subsides — perhaps the smart path is not — not to — press little matters — like the Portugal thing."

And Donovan had with an exasperated roar shut down the connection.

The next time Donovan called, and the time after that, there was no answer. He tried other means: a cell phone, a landline, an office line, email. When none of these worked, he'd called mutual friends and acquaintances. None of them knew where Freundhein was. None of them had heard from him for days.

That was yesterday.

Today, Mona was watching TV in the billiard room. She had built a little nest of blankets on an old armchair and — drinking directly from a pilfered bottle of chardonnay that a distracted Proud-boy had left in the dining hall — flipped on Hammer News. It wasn't her favorite, but it stuck with the news when the others switched format to prison exposé. More important, it was the one most directly attuned to the thoughts of the President and his Nation. And the communion of those

ODOACER

things, Mona understood, better than virtually anyone in the country, was the most important thing in the world at that moment.

The chyron read: "Storming the Beaches: Pres. to Rally in San Fran."

"What are you watching, Ms. France?"

Mona started. She had scarcely ever seen Donovan in this room before, and yet here he was, hovering in the doorway, as though waiting to be invited in. He was thinner, flesh hanging off his head in loose clumps, red-eyed, and he shook slightly when he spoke. He looked, above all else, sad.

"The news," Mona responded, almost feeling bad for the Lord of Trois-Fois-Maître, fallen in all but name. "Would you like to watch?"

"What's the story," he asked with a weak smile as he ambled into the room.

Mona gestured toward the old set. "Don't know. I just started watching. The President is having a rally."

"Yes," Donovan replied dreamily. "He likes those."

"In San Francisco."

"What?" Donovan stammered.

He stepped up to the set and turned up the sound.

"Surprise announcement from the President," said the newsreader as an image of the President trotting across the South Lawn to Marine One played on a loop. "The President saying he'd holding this rally on 'enemy territory' in hopes of rallying 'national unity' behind him. We're also hearing that the President will be heading to San Fran after attending a brief, private meeting in the seaside town of Tercero Maestro a few hours up the coast. That is off limits to the public and, we are told, may involve secret intelligence-gathering exercises of some description —"

Donovan shut off the TV. His lip quivered. He shook.

"Miss-miss-miss, Miss France," he stammered.

She met his eyes. They were watery. The former advisor's mouth hung agape and he said nothing.

ODOACER

"Are you okay, Mr. Donovan?" she asked at last.

"I must go," he blurted out. And then, with a swish of his golden-caped muumuu, Donovan was gone.

Mona sat up straight, thought just a moment, and knew then at once exactly what she must do. Abandoning all precautions, she raced to the trophy room, and then through the tunnels, to the control room.

Donovan was there, sweaty, out of breath, having arrived moments before she, and furious and afraid.

He was pigeon-typing now. Each letter in its own time, heralded by a firm, thoughtful poke at the keyboard: "Situations like this force me to stop and think about the people I have hurt. Worst of all, in private moments I worry that what drives me is not desire itself, but the unexamined need to be a kind of man I'm really not. Sad!"

Donovan paused. He read and reread what he had written. Mona could see the mouse hovering over the post button.

But Donovan just shook his head and erased what he'd written. His gaze returned to the little white ghosts on the screens.

One was watching the news and said to his son, "look at that: coming here to leach off our resources."

Donovan rubbed his hands together and typed: "We have to stop seeing the people who want to come here as the enemy. Most are hard-working and just want a chance to succeed. We all came here from somewhere!"

Donovan stared at these words for a few moments and then erased them, too.

The sound toggled to a faculty lounge somewhere. A coach held court with a too-eager English teacher, a 30-year-old-man, while the rest noticeably kept their distances. "We should be spending it here," yelled the coach.

"It's our money," said the teacher.

New words inched their way across the screen: "Foreign aid is a tricky issue. We need to allocate resources efficiently. But we mustn't lose sight of the fact we live in an

ODOACER

interconnected world and need friends." This too was erased, with a fanfare of angst, by the former presidential advisor.

Much was written. All was erased. Nothing was tweeted.

Peter S. Donovan, former presidential advisor, Lord of Trois-Fois-Maître, and father of his Nation, had lost his nerve. He collapsed in an undulating muumuu of man-sobs.

It was now only a matter of time before the President of the United States arrived in Tercero Maestro, California.

CHAPTER TWENTY-FIVE

CHARLES UNDERSTANDS HIS TRUE INTERESTS

Charles pouted in silence as Ezio drove him home from the Bernice's.

"Look, buddy, I'm sorry," said Ezio imploringly.

But Charles shot him a sour look that shut off the prospect of further conversation. Ezio instead fumbled with the radio until he'd found the local classic rock station — this one was called the Eagle — and turned it up. The song playing was one of those rock songs about being in a rock band — either Jukebox Hero or Shooting Star or Into the Great Wide Open or I'm Just a Singer in a Rock'n'Roll Band or American Band or Here I Go. Charles did his best to tune out the noise, and Ezio, until the car pulled up to his complex.

He stepped out, shut the door, leaned in the window, and glared.

"Look," said Ezio. "This is complicated for me."

Charles turned around and went inside.

Once he'd shut the door and waited for Ezio to drive away, Charles turned on his computer, opened it to his daily journal, and stared blankly at the screen.

ODOACER

The day had started so promisingly. The President's statements the evening before were surely the stuff from which Charles could teach Ezio — lovely, misguided Ezio — the true nature of His True Interests.

Specifically, what spewed out of the Presidential orifice was weird and discomfiting, drooling venom and bile across a range of seemingly random issues. None of the pundits or observers were quite sure why he chose that day, but choose it he did. And — much to Charles' satisfaction — at an impromptu news conference he went after: (1) the opposition party and the Quislings in his own party, some of whom he actually called "Quislings," for not approving the nominations of "pro-family" jurists without question and (2) the transgendered, who henceforth would be banned from the military, pending — as a much-later on-air clarification, evidently drafted by the White House legal team, made clear — review by the Defense Department and the Joint Chiefs.

It was, insofar as the Presidential ire was directed at segments of the LGBTQ community, of which he and Ezio were now secretly a part, a clear and convincing statement of national policy and priorities diametrically opposed to Ezio's true interests.

Charles met Ezio at the diner that morning. "I don't know what to think," he said as they sipped coffee at the counter. "The President seemed so promising on these — our — sort of issues during the campaign."

"What issues?" Ezio asked, absentmindedly.

"Did you see what he said this morning."

Ezio appeared nervous. He scanned the diner and talked in a low mumble. "Oh. Yeah, Andrew's gotta be totally triggering over that."

Charles gazed in astonishment at this comment. "But what about us?"

"Yeah," said Ezio after a pause. "Yeah, maybe we should talk about that later."

They hadn't talked about it later — either on the way to work, at work, or after work. They hadn't talked about it,

164

either, on the way to Bernice's, where they'd agreed to meet the guys for a drink that evening.

But the guys had talked about it. Exultantly. It was the first and last thing they wanted to discuss. The triggering! The owning! When the President's image appeared on a silent TV set above the bar, the guys demanded that Bernice turn up the volume, and she happily obliged. The report consisted of the Presidential pronouncements, the clarifying statement, and a pundit railing about the PC Police whose heightened sensitivities had driven the media to make a big thing of the situation. Finally, a statement from the White House to the effect that the President was serving the American People and American Families, and to do that needed effective judges and an effective military. This elicited nods of support from Bernice and the guys, all of whom swiftly lost interest in the whole affair.

But Charles, in his frustration, stepped out to the parking lot to look up at the moon and to smoke a cigarette. Ezio followed him out. They sat on the hood of the U.S.S. Thekla.

"What's wrong with you?" Ezio asked after lighting his own smoke.

"I don't know," replied Charles, knowing. "I feel — I guess — betrayed. You know, this stuff bothers me."

"Shit." Ezio smiled and slapped him on the back. "Shit, I wouldn't worry about that."

Charles spun on him. "Why not? He's coming after us — with his judges, with that ban. He's talking straight to the religious loons and they know exactly what he's saying to them."

Ezio chuckled mirthlessly. "Nah, I don't see it like that."

"How do you see it then?"

"Look," said Ezio, treading carefully. "This thing with you and me, I'm all for it. And, like, we can be open about it. Just not now, okay? But the guys will be fine with it. And, heck, society, now, is fine with it. The President's just triggering. You know, like, Andrew."

"Ezio Burgher, you know as well as anyone that I'm always in for some good, wholesome Andrew triggering. But this affects us. He's talking about policies. He's talking about lifetime appointments of civil servants with power over people's lives. This is real."

Ezio tossed out his cigarette and lit another. His eyes darted briefly to his open palm. "Nah, nah. I don't see it that way. It will be okay."

Then be put his arm over Charles shoulder and tried pulling him in closer. Charles resisted. "The thing is," Ezio said, "like this, this is fine. No one's complaining. But those guys, in the cities, they're in people's faces. People don't like that. And the media, and the — they're telling people how to think about it, and people don't like that either. And the President, well, he's just sticking up for the people." Ezio blew a smoke ring and watched it drift skyward until it encircled the moon itself. "He's sticking up for us."

"Bullshit!"

Ezio's countenance darkened and he all at once snarled. "Why do you hate him?"

"What do you mean, Ezio?"

Ezio stared into the darkness, back turned, and said nothing for several long moments. "Look," he finally spoke, "I never believed — well — I figured you were another reporter or something. Checking us out, getting the real story. You had the guys going, but. But I liked you Charles." His voice cracked. "I figured you wanted to teach me, so maybe I could teach you. But we can't teach each other."

Charles wasn't surprised. He didn't even care. "No," he said bitterly. "We can't."

"I love you," said Ezio, tearfully.

Charles had spoken to Ezio only once after that, and that was when he asked to be taken home.

166

ODOACER

And now he found himself staring at a laptop screen. He wanted to write something, but couldn't quite bring himself to form these words. Charles exhaled and finger-pecked a line:

T-h-i-s-[space]-i-s-[space]-w-h-a-t-[space]-t-h-e-y-[apostrophe]-r-e-[space]-i-n-t-e-r-e-s-t-e-d-[space]-i-n-[period].

Then he erased what he wrote.

He set the laptop aside and grabbed a small bowl that had been sitting on his TV table since breakfast. A shimmering of milk coated the bottom. He decided that he would be permitted to smoke indoors just this once.

All his adult life — since he was a teenager, really, since the dawning of his political consciousness — he thought, no, really believed, the problem was that people didn't understand their interests. Their True Interests. That, if they could be shown their interests, and made to see how they'd been tricked into caring about — about bullshit — then there'd be a reckoning. Superstructure, base, false consciousness, proletarian consciousness: before he'd been taught the vocabulary of Marxism, he had these ideas swimming around in his head, along with the conviction that people could only be tricked into evil.

And, since he started thinking this way, he saw a role for himself: he would be their teacher. He'd lay awake at night in high school, imagining the murals that would someday — perhaps soon — be painted of him on its walls. In these, he had a goatee and somewhat longer hair. And maybe he had a fist raised. They were all painted in gratitude to him for his insight and his willingness to share it. And they were painted out of a chauvinistic local pride in the fact that it all started here, in this high school.

It was the mark he'd leave on the world: the lifting of false consciousness, the un-tricking of the people.

And he didn't believe it anymore.

Charles Earl Jarlsberg III put out his cigarette in the cereal bowl and lit another. He hadn't smoked so much so fast in many years, and it tickled his throat. Judging the health risks

167

ODOACER

unwarranted, he put this second cigarette out, but soon after regretted this decision and lit a third.

He didn't believe anymore that the people could be taught Their True Interests because — and this made him saddest — because they weren't fucking idiots after all. They already knew Their True Interests. Their interests just weren't what Charles Earl Jarlsberg III wanted them to be.

People like Ezio and Bernice and the guys — they knew what they wanted. All the people in this town knew what they wanted. They wanted to live forever in a Grant Wood painting. They wanted to be greeted as equals by the bankers and the merchant, even, especially, if they were themselves ranch hands or miners. And vice versa. They wanted to be in church together. They wanted to know everyone at the diner. They wanted to be dignified, taciturn people who had guns to protect their homes and families.

And they wanted this to happen: if they encountered a black teenager on the street, or a Mexican one, or whatever, and if that teenager was doing something they saw as anti-social, and if in acknowledgement of this they rolled their eyes to Andrew — then, by god, they wanted Andrew to nod, or shake his head, or roll his eyes back. And if he couldn't do that — if he couldn't afford them that basic, baseline courtesy — if he had that little respect for his fellow citizen, and for the institution of citizenship — then, by god, fuck it, that fucking Andrew would have to be owned. That guy, Andrew, would have to be triggered.

They would drink Andrew's tears.

That was in their interests. That was Their True Interest.

And the other stuff — the medical care, the government services, the roads, the alliances, the breathable air, the unions, the rights — they weren't idiots. That was in their interests too.

It just wasn't as important.

Charles stood up and lugged his suitcase down from its shelf in the bedroom closet. He wouldn't even need to fill

ODOACER

it, he knew. He wasn't going to wear these clothes ever again. He wasn't going to the next town to continue his work. He'd move to the city and buy a decent wardrobe. To hell with it. He grabbed a few books, two pairs of jeans, a sweatshirt, socks, underwear.

He didn't need anything else. Not the plastic beer cups, not the NASCAR paraphernalia, not the classic rock CDs, not the frozen meals, nothing.

He gave the place one last look around, then opened the door.

And then his phone rang. It was Ezio.

"I'm leaving, Ezio," he said, and hung up.

The phone rang again. He accepted the call and hung up. It rang again.

"What, Ezio?"

Ezio's voice was hurried, even frantic. "I'm sorry about tonight," he said. "We can talk later. But, look, I'm calling everyone. I need to cal everyone. The call has gone out."

"What call?"

Ezio was panting in the other side, evidently in a tizzy, evidently packing up his own things, but for his own reasons. Because the call had gone out. "For the Red Hats," he finally said. "We're marching. Huge march. On San Fran. We're going to win one for the President. We owe him."

"Why are you calling me?"

There was a pause. "Because I want you to come see."

At that moment, the fog in which Charles had been laboring cleared abruptly. The world's edges became very sharp, the arc of history perfectly defined. His breathing, which had been rough after all the cigarettes, became crisp. The air filled him and lightened his mind. Charles Ear Jarlsberg III decided then that his work wasn't quite over. Not yet. He had one more mission to run.

"I'll pack," he lied. "When can you pick me up?"

ODOACER

Twelve hours later, Ezio and Charles sat in the back tier of 15-seat rental van heading north out of San Francisco International Airport on U.S. 101. The weather was clear to a point — a mass of fog hovered along the ridge to their left — and the traffic had been relatively light.

Neither had spoken to the other during the flight. They'd continued this after landing, allowing the guys to muddle through the van rental, and the setting of the GPS coordinates, in their own muddled way. At last the city had come into view, and the ticky-tack houses on the hillsides that had decorated the roadside till then gave way to larger-scale structures, modernized warehouses, new glass buildings, each a few stories high, bearing the names of famous technology firms. With that, the roadway had leapt onto high overpasses, and with that came traffic.

The van crept along. In the tier of seats ahead of them, Mickey had taken hold of Mikey's hand and was driving it repeatedly into the smaller man's prunish, mustachioed face as he taunted, "Stop hitting yourself, Mikey. Stop hitting yourself. Why are you hitting yourself?" A tier ahead of that, Scott and Obie laughed uproariously at these antics. And a tier ahead of that, giant Brian, with three seats to himself, slept. Ken in the driver's seat occasionally yelled for Mickey to shut the fuck up and for Mikey to quit hitting himself, but it seemed more a reaction to the traffic than to the self-hitting, and whenever the van moved again he laughed along. Bernice, in the front passenger seat, stared intently on her phone's GPS application and instantly repeated each instruction it gave, but in a more panicky tone of voice.

Charles looked to the right, chin on his hand. Ezio looked to the left, chin on his hand. One saw the bay, the other the hills.

"Look," said Ezio at last, quietly. The loud guffaws from the front seats had made it safe to talk. "Look, I'm sorry if I've been pissing you off somehow lately. But what the fuck has gotten into you? I can't even really figure out what you're

ODOACER

mad about. Isn't this what you wanted? To know what we're about?"

Charles spun to face his questioner, eyes smoldering. He had thought long and hard about what he would say now. And now he said it.

"Ezio, I will be very frank with you," he hissed. "I am a patriotic American. Same as you. I do not believe that the President has our best interests at heart."

Ezio angrily shushed him, but Charles wouldn't be put off.

"No, I will not shush. I have given you every benefit of the doubt. I have tried — very hard — to see and understand things from your point of view."

"And what?" snapped Ezio. "And what?" he repeated.

"And —" Charles was forgetting himself, forgetting his cover and the guys in front who still believed it. He knew it and he didn't care. "And I have tried explaining things to you, explaining them from every angle. And you don't care. You just don't care."

"About what?"

Charles didn't answer for several minutes. He struggled to bring his breathing under control, looked around at the city passing by, at the traffic, at the weather, which seemed to be taking a turn for the worse. Mickey and Mikey were still at it, to general acclaim. Bernice still echoed the GPS device's directions.

At last Charles turned to Ezio. He held back the tears he knew would come. "You don't care that the President is fucking us. You don't care that he's a liar and a bully. You don't care that he's a — he's a straight up criminal. You don't care that he won dishonestly, probably illegally, that he's a cheater. And possibly a traitor. And on top of all that, he is apparently batshit crazy."

Ezio gulped. He flinched. He blinked, like he was holding back tears. He was hurt.

171

ODOACER

"Charles," he said softly. "I care about — about all of that. You know I do. But, see? He lies — of course he lies — politicians lie — but he lies for us. He's a bully for us. Is a a crook? Sure. He's our crook: he does what needs to be done to protect us. He cheats for us. And if he's betraying anything, well, there's the law on one hand, and then there's the people. Us. He's batshit for us. He fights for us."

Charles was gobsmacked.

He fumbled for words. Then they came out in an almost babyish dribble of noise: "what about your kid, the river, fishing — what about us? You answer everything I said, but you didn't answer the part where I said he's fucking us. What about that?" The first tear coursed down his right cheek. "What about your — best interests?"

Ezio shrugged. "I told you, Charles. That all matters to me. But you can't get it all done at once, you know." His voice was soft, apologetic. He was reasoning things out, saying things aloud he'd not exactly thought through. But he said it with growing assurance. "You got to be realistic, you know? First things first."

"And what are the first things?" rasped Charles.

Ezio's answer was firm. It was tinged with sadness but it was, to him at least, loaded with inevitability. "Making America great again," he said. And into that answer was loaded every slight, every frustration, every betrayal. Andrew's failure to meet his eye roll, Andrew's ignoring a slob like him.

Into it was rolled the lost world of Mr. Rogers' Neighborhood, where Handyman Negri and Mr. McFeely, the delivery man, had their places, where they even had their titles.

That Charles had nothing to say in response was immaterial. At that very point, Mikey's plaintive whining — for he had now hit himself too hard — woke Brian, who, without so much as rubbing his eyes or stretching roared for the whole buncha goddamn f . . . — Brian, too, spoke presidentially sometimes — to shut the fuck up.

The whole bunch of them complied.

ODOACER

The fog had crept over the horn. Mist condensed on the van's windows. Charles watched it grimly. He was not sad or frustrated anymore.

That he had nothing to say in response to Ezio was immaterial. There was nothing to say in response. That was the whole point.

CHAPTER TWENTY-SIX

LANGEN MESSER

Former Presidential Advisor Peter S. Donovan arrived at lunch after his guests.

This was already odd. In days and weeks past, Mona and the Chevalier would arrive to find him lounging in his throne at the head of the table, smiling that somewhat amused, somewhat ironic smile of his, and bedecked in a silvery muumuu or in billowing space-age fabrics, or some such attire.

But that, too, was different today. When he came striding in after they'd already found their seats and started eating, he was disheveled, decked out in combat fatigues, and flanked on both sides by similarly clad Proud-boys. He looked like nothing so much as a Serbian war criminal, right down to his girth, his pallor, and the sculpted, '50s-style pompadour.

He forced a smile as he greeted his guests.

"Mona, good morning, charmed." She offered him her hand. He bowed low and kissed it, but the gesture was more mechanical than heartfelt. "Chevalier," he said, and the men exchanged curt nods.

Donovan took his seat and was served coffee. He ate nothing.

ODOACER

"Good Pete," said von Stilicho after some minutes had passed. He leaned back in his chair and picked at an ort of food with a toothpick. "Pardon me for being forward, but is something the matter?"

Donovan only smirked in response. This dissolved into a frown, then a glare.

"Mr. Donovan," Mona said cheerfully, "I will so miss our debates after we leave you."

The man's expression melted into a certain wistfulness. "As will I, my darling. But I hope you are not planning to leave me very soon."

"I am afraid we may have no choice, Mr. Donovan."

"And how is that?" asked the former presidential advisor with just a hint on indulgence.

Mona arranged her fingers into a neat tent shape, met her interrogator's gaze, and explained things patiently: "Well, it seems to me, Mr. Donovan, that certain things — certain things you have helped to bring about, perhaps — and that ought, in justice, be attributed to your rather unique genius — as I was saying, that these certain things have taken on a life of their own."

Donovan nodded. He plainly followed the gist of this nonsense.

"My dear Ms. France," he said, "what leads you to this conclusion."

"You will forgive me if my answer is somewhat abrupt, Mr. Donovan," she answered. "But as you may have already intuited, I am not completely ignorant of what is going on here." After reading the infinitely smug superiority — even under the present circumstances — that animated Donovan's smile, she added: "some of what's going on here."

"Go on."

"And it seems to me — how shall I put this? — that you have perhaps relied too much on the very assumptions you have so artfully — so, I might say, world-historically — subverted. And perhaps destroyed."

"And what are those, my darling?"

175

ODOACER

"Well, Mr. Donovan," said Mona France, "I suppose I mean, that you assumed that certain musty conventions — shame, perhaps — a certain striving for consistency — the aspiration to appear honest, or at least sane — or even the need to appear lawful — or not overtly criminal — that these conventions could contain a movement. A people on the move, I mean, in motion, I mean."

Donovan lowered his head. The apostle of the movement had, after all, misread or misunderstood the movement. And now this neophyte — not even a proper convert — was lecturing him about it.

"But it seems," Mona France continued, "it seems that all the quirks of character and temperament, all the will to action, that might embarrass, or compromise, or take down an ordinary constitutional officer are, in the leader of a great people, perhaps, seen — by the people, I mean — as rather admirable qualities."

Mona leaned in a bit.

"It seems, in other words, Mr. Donovan, that you are not in control of the situation anymore."

Whatever quavering would have, at that moment, overtaken the former advisor's already fragile demeanor, was erased at once — and replaced by a look of animalistic fierceness — as the end of Mona's speech was punctuated by a distant, but unmistakable, burst of machine gun fire. A half-moment later, the pounding of helicopter blades could be heard.

"You will excuse me," said Donovan with a grim smile. He walked out with his Proud-boys at his side. Mona and the Chevalier were alone. She looked to the strange little aristocrat, but he merely arched his eyebrow, flashed her an almost embarrassed grin, and stared dreamily into nothing.

"What do you suppose happens now?" she asked. There had been a few more bursts of gunfire and the helicopters were, judging by the noise, getting closer.

"Oh, I suppose we'll escape in some manner or another."

ODOACER

Outside, a klaxon began wailing. At the same time, inside the castle, soothing music — a combination of moog synthesizer, dulcimer, and a dulcetly howling wolf — filled the interior of the structure, punctuated at intervals by a calm English female's halting, disembodied voice, going "red alert . . . . this is a red alert . . . escape plan gamma initiated . . . red alert . . ."

Von Stilicho calmly stared into space, as before.

Mona tried taking some coffee, but was too distracted. She paced the room as the noise from outside grew louder and louder. Now, supplementing the more or less steady stream of small arms fire, the klaxon, and the inspirational evacuation recording, came competing music from outside. Loud, wailing guitars — heavy metal music. Mona knew at once that this was siege music. But she doubted very much that this would end up a siege.

She flung herself on the floor as a small rocket slammed into the castle wall just fifteen feet or so from the end of the dining hall. The room shook and the lights flickered. The Chevalier glanced back over his shoulder in a gesture of exaggerated annoyance but said nothing.

That rocket had come from the sea side, Mona realized.

She stood and peered out the window. The heavy thud of a chopper beat just out of view. And then it was in view — rising above the cliff's edge and the few straggly evergreen trees that clung to it.

It was an old-fashion style of contraption. The tail was a long, rectangular conglomeration of steel tubes, fitted together like an erector set. At the bottom were two large pontoons that appeared to have been fitted out with a variety of weapons. The cockpit was an oversized glass bulb, which afforded the astonished Mona France a very clear view of the vessel's pilot.

It was the President of the United States of America.

He was fitted out as always in orange spray tan, dark suit, and too-long red tie that fluttered in the strong eddies of

177

ODOACER

the turbine. He wore a red cap. Both hands rested on the control stick, forcing the man to hunch somewhat to avoid interference from his ample girth. He wore a look of fury, like in his official portraits, eyes — the irises a little too near the nose and too far from the ears — fixed on Mona.

She ducked again as the gatling gun affixed to one of the pontoons exploded in a continuous rat-tat-tat. The Chevalier ducked too. Both made their ways, on their bellies, inch by inch, to the far end of the room as the President's bullets shattered the window, and tore up the table, the chairs, the wall, the art, and the breakfast buffet.

Mona grabbed the door handle.

"It's locked!" she cried.

For a moment the cannonade ceased.

"Locked?" cried the Chevalier, shoving her gently aside and trying for himself. "Locked," he then said in astonishment.

Outside what was left of the room, the President's killer helicopter maneuvered to afford its pilot a better view of the interior. Mona hugged tight the Chevalier as the President's face came into view, as eye contact was made. The Chevalier held tight to her.

And the door swung violently open just as the guns erupted again. Mona and the Chevalier scudded into the hallway, then down a small flight of stair — they tumbled end over end — just in time to avoid being slaughtered by the President of the United States of America.

Looking up, they saw that the door, and the wall around it, had been replaced by a large hole over which the ceiling seemed to sag. They also saw the man who had opened it, and, in doing so, saved them.

It was former presidential advisor Peter S. Donovan.

He was cut, bruised, seemed to be bleeding, was definitely singed, and his uniform had been torn up and dirtied in many places. He was out of breath. In one hand he held a silver-plated revolver, which he waved about carelessly as he spoke. In the other, a phone. Mona could see it was opened

ODOACER

to the President's twitter page, and that another tweet was in mid-composition.

"Ms. France. Chevalier. You need to leave."

Neither answered.

"Take this," Donovan said, handing them a magnetic ID card that had dangled from his neck. "It will open every door in the place. Do you know where the garage is?"

Mona nodded.

"Go there. Don't bother trying by land. Or by sea. They have us surrounded."

"Then how — ?"

Donovan made an ironic smile and pointed up. "It seems you were right about many things, Ms France. Perhaps we can continue our discussions someday. I promise you, I have learned quite a lot. But now I must do as honor dictates."

Mona pointed to the phone.

"What are you typing?" she said.

"A tweet."

"From the President's account."

Donovan smiled grimly. "You know."

"I know."

"What does it say."

Donovan extended his arm, shakily, so the phone was right in her face. It was hard to focus, but the words gradually took shape:

"You are alone and scared and I can't fix it. You will always be alone and scared. I am just a crazy, sad man."

Mona and the former presidential advisor exchanged a long, strangely communal, look. For a moment, the cacophony of the unfolding military assault faded away.

"Are you going to send it?"

"I —" Donovan's voice cracked. "I don't know if I can."

"Send it," Mona said, gently.

"I."

"Send it," she said again.

"You have to go."

ODOACER

A nearby explosion shook the hallway, the roof of which partially collapsed into the space separating Mona and von Stilicho from their host. "Go!" Donovan cried.

As Mona and the Chevalier hurried down the hallway — the latter leading her by the hand as she looked back at her former host — she saw the former presidential advisor step through the new hole in the wall and into what had been the dining hall. A ruddy thumb dangled over the "post" button on his phone.

She heard three, then four distinct loud pops. Then she heard an effusion of gatling gun fire. Another pop, more fire. She never saw what happened.

Mona and the Chevalier wove through the corridors. Red emergency lights had switched on, and the ordinary lighting off. There was a hint of smoke in the air, then a taste of it in the mouth, a shock of it in the lungs. The small arms fire was getting closer, almost drowning out the soothing dulcimer-wolf music that urged calm reflection of the evacuees. From a colonnaded landing, Mona could see, in the large entryway below, actual real-life fire fighting. The Proud-boys, shooting desperately from isolated positions behind suits of armor and stuffed livestock, were getting the worst of it. She counted two, three, five down, and then two more were killed right in front of her. A large tapestry to the right of the door had caught fire.

The assailants wore black commando gear with what seemed to be military insignia on their shoulders. Balaclavas covered their faces and, there, on their heads, were the caps. The red caps.

The soldiers were wearing red caps.

Another Proud-boy went down. A rocket-propelled grenade slammed into the grand staircase, causing a flight of stairs to come crashing down. This started another fire. The air was pungent, and filled with — in addition to the gunfire and the dulcimer-wolf music — the screams of dying men.

They were the first and last sounds Mona ever heard coming from the outmatched Proud-boys.

ODOACER

"Come, Mona," said the Chevalier. She went.

They raced down a long passage, using the card key as they went to breeze through a series of security checkpoints. A right at the chandelier, down a flight, and at last they were at the large, featureless steel door that, until now, had kept them out of the garage. Not anymore. It only opened halfway when they swiped the card — apparently the motor room was under assault as well — but this gave them room enough to slip through.

The garage was eerily quiet. The thick walls muffled the sounds outside. The lights had gone out, and it was dark but for a large skylight, which lay directly above the hot air balloon. The balloon itself had already been inflated, and had on its side a garish rainbow pattern. The Chevalier headed straight for it.

"What?" exclaimed Mona. "The balloon?"

Of course, she had known it would come to this. It was still weird.

"We really have no other choice," said the Chevalier, unspooling one mooring line, then another, from the heavy steel cleats in the floor of the garage. Mona was prepared to get into it with the Chevalier on the topic of choice, but before she could he leapt into the balloon's wicker gondola. As he loosened a sheet, the balloon began to lift, first a foot off the floor, then a few more. The Chevalier leaned over the side and held out his hand. "Come, Mona."

Without another thought, she went. She hopped a bit, the Chevalier pulled, and with a thud she landed in the bottom of the basket.

"Trust me," said the Chevalier, through clenched teeth. He had righted himself and held a rope — a sheet, as balloonists call it — in his mouth. With his hands he adjusted the flame of the burner. "I am, after all, a world-renowned professional balloonist."

Mona had not known this fact about von Stilicho. But it did not altogether surprise her, either, once she allowed for a world that contained professional balloonists, and even

ODOACER

professional balloonists of renown. In that context — which the reader knows is the true and correct context — the Chevalier's claim made almost perfect sense.

The balloon lifted — out of the garage and then, with surprising swiftness, over the property. It probably had less to do with the Chevalier's professionalism as a balloonist, and more to do with the more pressing matters at hand, that the attackers did not seem to notice two human beings escaping from a seaside castle in a garishly colored hot air balloon. But whatever the reason, they didn't. They were busy.

They swarmed over the property.

Like the raiders Mona had seen in the entryway, they wore black military uniforms and the red hats. One could follow from their positions, and their positions throughout the grounds of the complex, the general thrust of their assault. Five military tanks had evidently smashed through the main gate and gone right up to the front door, which appeared to have been blown open. Discarded parachutes lay strewn about the complex at various points, including one or two for which the unlucky paratrooper had become ensnared on a tree or on one of the castle's turrets or antennae. These hung limply from their cords. As the balloon blew slightly out to sea, Mona could observe rappelling cables going up the high cliff — these must have been 500 feet — and on some of these still dangled the commandoes. A small flotilla of ships waited out at sea. Black helicopters — and one presidential helicopter — buzzed the grounds relentlessly, emitting bursts of machine gun fire from time to time. The President's chopper seemed to be engaged in this endeavor with more diligence than the others.

Mona flinched as she observed small groups on Proud-boys rounded up by the red capped commandoes and, in twos and fours, lined up against the castle walls and summarily executed. There was no sign of Donovan, but the castle itself was engulfed in flame on two sides. The stately dining hall, Mona could see, had been completely obliterated, and the gardens where she had enjoyed many cool afternoons were strewn with rubble.

ODOACER

As the balloon caught a thermal, swinging the gondola abruptly to the east, Mona gripped the rail and became momentarily nauseated. The Chevalier grinned broadly. "Won't you fly in my beautiful balloon?" he sang.

There was a faint orgy of gunfire below as five more Proud-boys were executed. At about that moment, the south tower of Trois-Fois-Maître, which had been built 400 years earlier and withstood wars of religion, revolution, and national unification before it was boxed up, shipped to California and meticulously reassembled, crashed in a effusion of ash and flame into the Pacific Ocean.

"Up, up and away," the Chevalier sang, "in my beautiful, my beautiful balloon!"

The   balloon   wafted   south.

CHAPTER TWENTY-SEVEN

SCENES FROM THE OCCUPATION

Charles groused, only these philistines could plan a rally in San Francisco and choose Fisherman's Wharf. But in fact the sea of red hats stretched much further than that — all down the Embarcadero and up the streets climbing Russian Hill. That sea merged with the real sea: party boats full of them bobbed carelessly in the bay while jet skis with red-hatted riders weaved between and betwixt them. Someone, a Silicon Valley group, had chartered a larger cruising vessel, and the decks of this, too, were thronged with red-hatted tech bros.

The mood among the crowd was jubilant, triumphant. Many had already taken to drink. Many more cradled flag poles under their arms, carrying their full-size flags. Many a sentimental tear emerged from under the lip of many an aviator glass lens and dribbled down many a bronzed cheek. Horns were honking, classic rock booming.

The locals had mostly taken to their homes, Charles noted. Stores were shuttered. What proprietors had thought to make a quick buck off the event were no doubt regretting it now that — two hours after the scheduled start of festivities

ODOACER

without an appearance by, or even a word from, the President — bar tabs were going unpaid and T-shirt stands were being surreptitiously looted. The police presence was large, but the goal today was of necessity keeping the peace, not law enforcement, and any transgression short of violence — of which there was much — would go unpunished.

Charles was speaking to Ezio, but barely. He'd limited conversation to the restrained, polite, and informative. Which way do we go here? Take a right. When does this start? It was supposed to have started at . . . and so on. Mickey and Mikey both had gotten blisteringly drunk and had dozed off under a tree while enjoying a Journey tribute band, playing the outdoor area of a tourist bar across the street. Brian was uncomfortably close, but the rest of the guys were, for the moment, lost in the crowd.

Charles sipped a water bottle, tried to tune out the crowd, and plotted out his next move.

There was a buzzing in his pocket. There was a buzzing in every person's pocket. So much buzzing, the whole world seemed to buzz. And everyone looked down, all the Red Hats who crowded the "enemy territory" of San Francisco. And everyone took a device from his or her pocket and looked at it. Some punched in codes, some scanned their thumbs, some had their devices already out. They all looked. Every brow was, for a moment, covered in the black shadow of a red bill of a red hat. Every set of eyes was focused on tweet.

A tweet from the President's twitter account.

It said:

"Huge win today for me and for America! This is for real! This is for real me. I will address my fans in San Francisco soon. Stay tuned."

And, before the Red Hats had finished reading that tweet, there was another buzzing. Another tweet. They read that one too. It said:

ODOACER

This is really me. We have made so
much progress and have so much to do.
Will outline my plans in San Fran later
today. God bless America. NATIONAL
RESTORATION!

No one there that day, none of the Red Hats, really
knew what to make of it. But they knew, in case some of them
hadn't already, that the man addressing them on the twitter
machine was real.

He was the real thing.

CHAPTER TWENTY-EIGHT

SURRENDER TO PASSION

Whatever the prevailing winds are in northern California on an ordinary day, on this day they were carrying our protagonists south along the coast toward San Francisco. Mona watched the world pass along below: the green coastal hills, gradually succumbing in hues of brown and yellow to the onrushing summer months, the towering spongy rock and the surf below, the specks signifying the grazing locations of the fat, lazy cattle, cars, trailers, homes.

After this thrilling landscape had become monotonous, she lifted her gaze to her traveling companion, the small, mysterious nobleman whose every movement had infuriated her, and who yet remained so inscrutably sure of himself. He was trimming the balloon's sheets as though he knew how — though Mona wasn't at all sure that he did.

"You never had anything to say to Donovan," she said at last. He looked to her as though surprised and hastily hitched the sheet he'd been pulling on. "I mean, when he was ranting about Pakistanis," she continued. "Or trying to goad me into discussing his so-called nation."

"I had nothing to say to him," said the Chevalier. It was to Mona's surprise that, for once, he did not appear to be trying to convey a tone of general mirth. She had taken this to be characteristic of all his utterances, from the most insipid to the most grave. Yet here he was perfectly matter of fact.

"But he was wrong about — so many things."

"There's nothing to be gained by debating a person like Pete," the Chevalier replied in a tone that was not grim, but was not quite conversational either. "You wanted to hear what he had to say. There — you heard it. Perhaps you even found some of his ideas about shirtless stevedores a bit compelling."

That there was some truth to this, she was unwilling to reveal. Instead, she stared daggers at her balloon-mate. Or attempted to.

"On an intuitive, emotional level, I mean," he continued. "But that's exactly the point. How do you argue with a sentiment, with nostalgia? How do you argue with a Grant Wood painting or a half-remembered Fourth of July picnic? You don't." The Chevalier frowned.

"What do you do then?"

"Well, Mona, at some point or another, you fight." He shrugged his shoulders and turned again to the sheets.

Mona pondered his words a moment, then grabbed his shoulders and gently — more by suggestion than by force — spun him around to face her.

"For what?" she asked.

Something in Donovan's ideology of nostalgia had bothered her. It was this: There was, as the Chevalier stressed, no answer to it. In its own way, it was all on rock-solid foundations: a view of history that, if it did not correspond exactly to reality, corresponded to people's image of reality. It was felt.

And were people crazy to feel things once felt better? It didn't matter if they were crazy. They felt. Their felt belief in Donovan's mythic past and glorious future — their will to make America great again — had a kind of reality of its own.

ODOACER

And against this, thought Mona, what? An abstract and dehumanized humanism? Categories without content? Ideals moored one day in natural right, the next in social utility, and the next day not ideals but some kind of scientific necessity. What do we have, but . . . ?

The Chevalier, who perhaps needed sometime to answer the question Mona asked out loud, answered the question she thought.

"A chance to build our own thing in the world," he said.

"What?"

"We fight for a chance to build our own thing in the world."

Inspired, Mona said, "let's bang again."

"I thought you'd never ask," said the Chevalier. And they promptly did. It was weird in a balloon, but also kind of thrilling — at least for Mona, who was not a world-renowned professional balloonist and who could not say she'd ever done anything like this before. The thrill made up, this time, for the Chevalier's not-especially-generous approach to love-making. Positions were tried, things attempted, et cetera, et cetera. And the usual descriptors applied: heaving, panting, aching, sweaty, moaning, gasping, crescendoing and what not.

When it was over, the Chevalier promptly fell asleep in a corner of the basket, either confident the winds would take them where they needed to go — wherever that was — or not caring where they wound up.

Mona threw on some clothes: the Chevalier's shirt, buttoned a couple times in the middle just to give things the appearance of decency. She folded her arms over the rim of the basket and again took in the view.

They were clearing the Marin highlands and drifting south parallel to the Golden Gate Bridge. By the look of things, they would make landfall on the west side of the Presidio. It was a starkly beautiful afternoon. The sun shone, there was a light breeze stirring up little white caps on the bay, and the air was clear, the fog having beat a retreat to the far

ODOACER

horizon. The city gleamed. But it looked different. Gone were the para-sailors and para-boarders and yachters who ordinarily packed the bay on days such as this. Instead, a multitude of jetskiers — with what looked like little red heads — wove through a multitude of party boats. The roads were also unusually empty, empty of cars, and, to the extent one could tell at this distance, empty of bikes and pedestrians too. There was a throng of red at the waterfront, but very little life beyond that. A shriek overhead heralded a formation of fighter jets, each trailing behind it a puff of red- or white- or blue-dyed exhaust. There were helicopters too, military helicopters, hovering low over different parts of the city, and of the bay generally. And, Mona now saw, heading south on the bridge, a convoy of military vehicles: tanks and armored cars. Men in black sat and stood triumphantly on the hoods and in the turrets, all in red hats. They were waving flags. It was the party that raided Troi-Fois-Maître, returning to the captured enemy city of San Francisco in triumph. They were honking, blaring music — the same classic rock siege music they's blasted at the raid — hooting, hollering, and gesticulating.

And then Mona France heard something behind her, getting louder. A whirl. A certain persistent thudding. She spun with a start to see the source.

It was the President's personal attack helicopter. And it was bearing down on them.

"Chevalier!" Mona shouted. "Chevalier!" She gave him a kick. "Ritter."

The Chevalier stirred. Groggily, squintily, he grinned. "Ritter is a title, darling. Like Chevalier. It's German for rider."

"O my god, shut up."

The Ritter lifted his head and looked around. "Are we there yet?" he asked, as though they had been going anywhere besides away from the burning castle.

190

ODOACER

"I think we're in trouble," said Mona, gesturing toward the attack chopper. It was gaining fast. You could now see the whitish patches under the president's eyes.

"I think that's the President," said the Chevalier.

"Yes, it's the President, dumbass. And he's gaining on us."

Twin spouts of flame erupted from the ends of the pontoons. The president was still out of range, but he'd given them a terrible glimpse of what was coming.

The Chevalier arched his eyebrow, as was his wont, and, without great fuss, stood up and began putting on his pants. The President meanwhile made a couple more shows of pyrotechnics. The flames licked closer each time.

"Aren't you going to do anything?" Mona screamed, forgetting, perhaps, that she was addressing a world-renowned professional balloonist who of course knew better than she did how best to evade a flame throwing attack helicopter piloted by a vengeful United States President.

"Patience, my dear," he said. "Ritter and Chevalier— they're pretty much the same word, you know. Just in different languages. It's similar to the Spanish caballero." He rubbed his thin. "I'm afraid it's not very economical to be a Chevalier Ritter von Stilicho." And then he threw hack his head and laughed gaily. "Ah-hah! Ah-hahahaha!"

"Chevalier!"

Lightning-fast, von Stilicho leaned over the burner and cut the flame. He then tugged swiftly on some sheets that, it seemed, had the effect of wringing some of the hot air out of the balloon. Mona felt her stomach turn.

The balloon sank precipitously as the President soared impotently overhead, burning to plasma the spot of air they'd previously occupied.

The Chevalier winked.

"We're not out of the woods yet!" Mona hollered.

And they weren't. The chopper banked in a wide right turn. It was coming back, quick. And now the President had the drop on them.

"Strap on that parachute, would you?" The Chevalier pulled two from the netting on the inside of the basket, slung one over his shoulders, and began buckling in. Mona followed suit. "Very good, love."

The Chevalier waited for one second, two seconds, three — and —

"Now!" he exclaimed. With what seemed like a single gesture, he opened the flame on the burner full throttle, cut the ballast from the basket, grabbed Mona, and propelled the two of them out of the basket and into the ether.

Mona couldn't even gasp. It all seemed to her unreal.

There was no sound. The Chevalier was still holding onto her — a little too close, perhaps, but she'd let that go. The bay, and the earth, were getting closer. And the balloon, above, was getting further away. It wasn't just their rapid descent. With the ballast gone — including their ballast — and the burner on full, it rose abruptly. . .

Right into the path of the onrushing chopper.

The balloon and its rigging instantly became entangled in the rotors. That alone might have taken down the helicopter, but the balloon at once evaporated in a silent puff of flame. This in turn appeared to ignite the tanks feeding the flame throwers, the fuel lines, and all the various munitions the dread craft carried.

And then the sound came back.

A loud pop.

The Presidential attack chopper was gone.

Heavy breathing. Hers, the Chevaliers.

She reached for the ripcord. He patted her hand away. "Not yet," he said, gently, but at the top of his lungs.

Her eyes widened.

"Look," she screamed, pointing up.

The Chevalier looked up.

Bearing down on them like a missile was the President of the United States. His hair, his too-long tie, and his ill-fitting suit fluttered in the onrush of atmosphere. He had made himself torpedo-shaped, but would occasionally flap his

ODOACER

arms, as though swimming the breast stroke, and each time he did he seemed to gain on them.

His face was a mask of pure rage, similar to the glare he wore in his official portraits. But his eyes said nothing.

The Chevalier smiled and, perhaps taking a minor liberty, gave his lover a light peck on the cheek. "Time to say goodbye, for now," he said, and before she could respond, he yanked her ripcord.

Mona France felt a tremendous jolt. Her shoulders and upper back jerked up, then her lower body followed suit. Her arms hurt. She saw spots. The chute opened. She was floating.

She could only watch from increasing distance what happened next.

The President caught the Chevalier.

A mid-air kung-fu fight ensued in which each held his own surprising well.

The parachute was pulled from the Chevalier's shoulders.

The men fought over it, each landing a few well-aimed kicks on the other's testicles without either letting go of the prized chute.

And then both disappeared into a thin wisp of cloud that, drifting out of lockstep with the fog, had decided to tarry over the Presidio.

CHAPTER TWENTY-NINE

THE VICE PRESIDENTIAL JET PACK IS STOLEN

The whole operation was in free-fall.

What idiocy, it thought. They had just become masters of Their fate, and what did they do with it? They impetuously got in a helicopter crash.

It couldn't help paying attention, now, to the contingencies, the ephemera, the un-eternal, the finite. Like the finite amount of space between the man and the ground. Would it end thus?

But They still had fight in Them.

Or so it seemed, until the dark little man, with one last swift kick in the man's balls, caused the man to let go of the chute for a split second. The dark man then kicked off the man, giving him just enough space to strap on the chute — perhaps inadequately — and pull the ripcord. And then the dark man was no longer falling next to the man. He appeared to be falling up. But that wasn't really what was happening.

The man was falling down.

It wondered about things.

ODOACER

What made Them think They should be in charge? What made Them think They were better than the Plan? What folly.

And what about it? What about me?

Am I the eternal living principle, or soul, in him? Is that all I am?

And am I going to die?

The ground was getting awfully close. The grass on which the operation would most likely go splat was browning. The paths were empty of strollers, save for the occasional dog walker. The sea, not far away, was blue and beautiful. The sun glinted off it.

Who were They anyway? Was I asleep?

It thought about time, about its time, and how it seemed to begin when the man's time began, and how it seemed to always unfold from the man's point of view. Surely, time was happening everywhere else as well, it now thought, but time always seemed to be, uniquely, ours.

It could make out distinct trees. A stunted, new-growth coastal redwood. A grove of sickly, invasive eucalyptus. Bushes — it didn't know botany all that well — but pretty bushes in full bloom with pink flowers.

It had warm memories, and its warm memories were the man's warm memories. Not abstract contemplations of god and the infinite, not transcendence, but little pictures. Of the man's mother and father, even of his brother. Of pets. Of places. Of — were they called friends? Of children. Of Christmases. Children at the tree, little red hats, not those red hats but nice red hats, squirming through church, all those aunts and uncles, some drunks some not, now all dead.

Merry Christmas, it thought. We can say Merry Christmas again, right?

The world rushed closer and closer and closer.

Merry Christmas! Merry Christmas! Merry Christmas you wonderful old Savings and Loan!

It was about to be over.

And then it wasn't.

195

ODOACER

A pair of hands — spindly and white — seized the man's upper arms from behind. They held tight. At first, they fell together. Then they slowed together, evened out together, careened parallel to the earth together, perhaps a hundred feet up. Veered right in a wide arch together. Soared over the bay together. They were flying.

The man must have looked up. It could see who was had saved them.

It was the Vice President. He wore a neat blue suit that, as usual, perhaps overemphasized his shoulders, and neither that nor his snow-white, close-cropped hair was at all disturbed. The Vice President wore a jetpack.

His face wore the usual expression of intense concentration masking, or attempting to mask, utter vacuity.

He neither said anything nor smiled, but his eyes opened just a bit, exposing parts of the whites that shouldn't be exposed, seeking praise.

They were evidently in no mood to give it.

"Give me the pack, Mike," said the President of the United States. "You get off here."

The Vice President started.

"Mr. President?"

"I said I need the pack."

"But I rescued you. I can take you to safety."

"Not yet, Mike," said the man. "I'm not done. I'm going to catch those fuckers."

The Vice President opened his mouth as if to say something — perhaps to ask who the fuckers were and why they needed to be caught, perhaps to raise a protest, although that was unlikely. Most likely, he wanted to say something colossally dignified and appropriate, like, it's been an honor to serve in your administration. But after surveying the man's face, he simply began unstrapping himself from the jetpack.

The precise sequence of maneuvers by which one man transfers a jetpack to the man he's carrying, mid-flight, though familiar to the enthusiast, are extremely technical and difficult to describe to the casual reader. There are manuals and

ODOACER

perhaps online instructional videos that provide an idea of how it works. It suffices to say that these maneuvers were conducted efficiently, offered a suitable spectacle, and, when they were complete, the President of the United State was soaring over San Francisco Bay in a jetpack, and the Vice President of the United States was falling end-over-end into San Francisco Bay, where he fortunately splashed down without injury and was rescued by an only moderately drunk jet-skier.

It could feel Them roar, all of them. The man was roaring too. And it was roaring too.

CHAPTER THIRTY

KING OF KINGS

"What's that, Charles?"

Ezio was pointing. A lot of people were pointing.

Shading his eyes with a rolled-up event schedule, Charles looked where they were pointing. It was like nothing he'd ever seen.

Far out over the bay — past the party-boats and thronging jet skiers, past the chartered mega-yachts — a small speck. A small, flying speck.

It was a man. A man with a jetpack.

He was too far away to see well. He seemed large, rather wide, and he seemed to be wearing a suit with a too-long tie, and to have a wild mass of hair flopping around his temples like a halo. The jetpack was blasting full-bore, emitting behind it a furious trail of flame and smoke.

The man dropped to about 20 feet above the bay and hovered a moment. The exhaust pummeled the surface, sending forth powerful ripples for which the more sober jet-skiers set off with alacrity. But when they reached the source of the ripples, or got near enough, the jet-skiers stopped and

ODOACER

looked up in what must have been astonishment. They bobbed in the surf. Their arms went up — some went in pumped fists, some merely went up. Charles could hear their cheers, their rising cheers, their insane cheers, from where he stood.

And the jet-skiers parted before the man with the jetpack. And, no doubt informed of something miraculous by those close at hand, the party boats came about to create a path. As each did — as each crew learned the news — what news? — the roar grew louder, louder, and louder still.

And once the path was cleared, the man with the jetpack stopped hovering. He leaned forward, made himself parallel with the ground, and revved up his jets still more. A flower of orange and red and yellow flame exploded behind him. There was a pop — a sonic boom? And the man was headed straight for the shore. Straight for Charles.

The exhaust, and the man's sheer speed, created a heavy wake in which the jet-skiers and party boats bobbed again. There were gales of laughter — ecstatic, childish laughter — as each wobbled and was drenched in the spray.

The man shot over the shore, over the crowd, over Charles' head. And the roar became thunder. Sustained, abandoned, euphoric, triumphant, thunderous noise.

For flying over the assembled Red Hats, the faithful Red Hats, the indomitable, never surrendering, wild and crazy Red Hats, the bestriders of the earth, in a jet pack — a shiny jetpack belching out all-incinerating red and orange exhaust — was the President of the United States of America.

He wore the expression he always wore in his official portraits, Charles was surprised to find himself thinking. That intense, angry scowl. Those fixed, staring eyes. The downturned lips. Like an angry grocer.

It was the look, he couldn't help thinking, of a protector, a champion, a hero. It was a man out to slay evil.

And, apparently, he was out to slay it right now. The President shot overhead and up one of the side streets to Russian Hill.

ODOACER

He was after something. And, whatever that something was, Charles knew, he had to help it.

While the throngs of Red Hats gaped in religious astonishment, Charles took off in the same direction as the President.

He hardly noticed that Ezio followed.

CHAPTER THIRTY-ONE

A CAR CHASE, FINALLY

Mona France alit gently on a browning clump of grass not far from the Golden Gate Bridge. It was quiet here. Traffic was light, foot traffic lighter. She did not ache. Nothing hurt. Her breathing was regular.

She unbuckled the chute and let the emptied pack fall to her ankles, then kicked the whole apparatus discreetly out of the way under an immature eucalyptus.

The world here had a quiet, alien quality. The light was too bright, her bones too tired, her skin too sunburned, her pores salty and sweat-clogged. A gentle, damp breeze stirred from the sea. It was the kind of feeling one had, say, after a long hike — tired and satisfied, looking forward to a shower and then maybe a beer or six at an outdoor bar, and then an early bedtime. She felt good.

A horn honked shrilly behind Mona France.

She turned abruptly, only to see the Chevalier Ritter von Stilicho seated behind the wheel of a nifty Mazda Miata, English racing green. He smiled at her and then beeped again.

"Come along, Mona," he cried, cheerfully. "Our work is not yet done."

She got in.

"Where did you get the car?"

The Chevalier merely winked in response. Mona didn't press him. She was sure the answer in some way, shape or form was seduction, but she neither wanted to know how this was accomplished in the few extra minutes it must have taken her to drift to the surface, nor wanted to contemplate the little aristocrats somewhat loose sexual mores. She did, however, manage to look away when he leaned in to kiss her.

"You're alive," she said robotically.

"For now, it appears," said von Stilicho, staring the engine and turning toward the city.

"The President? The Chevalier thought for a moment, then accelerated. "I think he must have made it. I should imagine I'd have seen the wreckage when I landed."

Mona shook her head. "Are you saying he can fly now?"

"I'm saying, Mona France, that this is an unconventional chief executive."

Mona then noticed how fast they were going.

The sparsity of street traffic eased the way, but, even so, the Chevalier was really pushing the limits of the Miata's motor. As this was San Francisco, the little car lurched into the air a few feet each time it crested a hilltop.

"Where are you going, Chevalier? Where are you going in such a hurry?"

The Chevalier offered a wistful smile, but kept his eyes on the road. "I'm afraid it's no longer safe for us here. We shall have to go to ground. I have a place in Chinatown. One we're there, we can figure out what comes next. How to reconnect with my taciturn Jørgen."

"What do you mean what comes next?" Mona snapped. "We need to get what we know to the public. Donovan, the twitter account, the attack on the castle, the executions. Chevalier, we know Donovan was manipulating the President for years in order to bring fascism to America! This needs to get out."

The Chevalier shook his head sadly and let Mona's words hang in the air. Then he said: "Yes, Mona. I suppose there will be time for all of that. And I suppose it might make a difference to some people."

"To some people?" There was a tear, just a hint of a tear, in her voice.

"Who knows, Mona? Maybe more. But for now we must survive." The Chevalier depressed the accelerator still further. The city whizzed by.

They were topping Russian Hill. The nondescript tan low-rises, which would have been at home in, say, Osaka or Fort Lee, had given way to stately Victorians, dolled up in pastel colors, but unwelcoming today.

"Oh my!" cried the Chevalier.

"Oh my what?" said Mona.

The car slowed. There were people in the street, many signs urging cautious driving.

"It seems we have come to the zig-zaggy part of Lombard Street," the Chevalier reported meekly.

"What?" Mona lifted herself up almost onto the back of her seat and peered out over the top of the Miata's windshield. The road abruptly disappeared into nothing ahead of them as heads — tourists heads — bobbed this way and that both on and over the edge of the precipice. They had, as the aristocrat warned, reached the infamous zig-saggy part of Lombard Street.

This is a place where the escarpment of Russian Hill was too steep for a regular through-street but where the undaunted engineers installed a series of sharp switchbacks that, for a city block, lead vehicles safely down the slope. These switchbacks are flanked on both sides by extremely expensive homes with small but neat patios, each abutting one of the interior angles of the roadway, which are fussily masoned and used for parking and gardening.

The Chevalier leaned on the horn as hard as he could and revved the engines, setting the tourists scrambling. But there was only so much he could do. There were cars in front of him, chancing the zig-zags for a few seconds of very boring home video, and there was really nothing to do but follow them. "Is there nothing you can do?" imported Mona.

The Chevalier leaned on the horn again, eliciting a stern "fuck you" from someone further up the queue.

"Okay, fine. Stop beeping." Mona whisked his hand from the horn. "It doesn't help. Stop."

Von Stilicho snuck in one last beep.

"Okay, stop. Okay? Just be cool and wait."

The Chevalier shrugged his shoulders and turned on the radio. After flipping through a few stations, he found a song to his liking, I've Got the Power, the 1990 techno anthem by German Eurodance troupe Snap!

"Okay," said Mona. "Good. Listen. Sing along." The Chevalier was in fact singing along, but only to the guitar—"Da-Da-Da da da"—and to the refrain—"I've got the Power!" He beat his hands on the steering wheel. "I don't see what the hurry is anyhow."

And then, on cue, the President of the United States appeared in a jetpack.

He was directly above the intersection of Leavenworth Street and Lombard, which is to say at the bottom of the zig-zaggy part, but hovered about 100 feet above it, putting him almost on level with his prey.

"Chevalier?"

"I see him," replied the aristocrat, turning up the volume on the stereo. He slammed on the gas.

The car careened over one of the interior angles, decapitating a topiary and annihilating a brick retaining wall before landing on top of a parked Lexus.

DA-DA-DA DA DA. I've Got the Power!

The Chevalier beeped furiously, dispersing tourists this way and that and the Miata returned to the pavement.

DA-DA-DA DA DA. I've Got the Power!

The President lurched forward with an explosion of yellow sparks, and, with an unintelligible roar, depressed the red buttons atop the jetpack's control levers. These activated small laser cannons mounted on either side of the pack's headrest.

Each blast landed like a grenade against the escarpment of Lombard Street. Into the sides of cars, collapsing porches, obliterating walls and gardens, felling terrified people. There were screams, booms, crashes, honking horns, cried, moaning. The barrage continued as the President continued roaring.

DA-DA-DA DA DA! I've Got the Power!

The Chevalier hung a hard right, again cutting an interior angle. This time the Miata careened through four zig-zags, ruining all in its ill-fated path: more topiaries, more retaining walls, a marble bench, more cars, and a nice terra cotta flower urn.

DA-DA-DA DA DA! I've Got the Power!

The President kept firing. Cars were blasted into the air. Deep craters formed. Fires started.

DA-DA-DA DA DA!

"Hold onto something Mona!" yelled the Chevalier.

"What!?" Mona braced herself against the dash. The Chevalier floored the gas pedal.

"ARRRRRRR!" screamed the President.

BLAM-BLAM-BLAM went the jetpack-mounted laser cannons.

VROOOOOOOOOOM went the engine.

I've Got the Power!

The Miata hurdled into the air. For the time it was there, it seemed, to Mona, to be floating in slow motion.

It missed the flying President by mere feet, passing in momentary safety while the chief executive's face contorted in rage.

DA-DA-DA DA DA!

And then the Miata crashed to the surface. It crashed, then it flipped, then it skidded on its roof and spun, and then it hit a wall on the far side of Leavenworth, its front becoming embedded in the brick.

ODOACER

As the radio sputtered and died, Mona France heard only the eerily fading final lines of Snap!'s dancehall opus. They went, *sotto voce*, "I've Got the Power!"

And then all was quiet.

CHAPTER THIRTY-TWO

EZIO HAS SECOND THOUGHTS

Charles saw the flying President descend behind a cluster of buildings, reemerge on the far side of an apartment tower, and then disappear again into a cluster of trees. A moment passed, followed by a series of crashes and several plumes of smoke rising skyward. He never stopped running toward the scene.

He found them at the bottom of that stretch of Lombard Street with the sharply zig-zagging roadway. A straighter, steeper path had evidently been bulldozed through the mid portion of the hill. The triangular gardens, occupying the interior angles of the roadway, had been demolished. Chunks of brick lay everywhere, along with what looked like bodies, and there were fires. Many little, and for now contained, fires creeping up bush and vine to the buildings' facades. Several home security alarms wailed, and several people too, while the rotors of a helicopter — perhaps of two helicopters, thudded ever louder.

At the bottom of the hill — or of the part of the hill with the zig-zagging — an overturned Mazda Miata lay prone, its rear wheels still spinning, its crumpled front half-embedded in the side of a porch. Its engine was on fire. And a woman — Mona France — Charles recognized her from a portrait photograph enclosed in Hanno's envelope — appeared to be pulling an unconscious man — Hanno! — away from the wreckage. Above them hovered the President of the United States of America in a jetpack.

The straps pinched his torso a bit, having evidently been adjusted for a more slender set of shoulders, forcing the fat of his midriff to bubble forward in a manner that strained the front buttons of his shirt. His head was leaned back over the jetpack's headrest, such that he watched his prey through the bottoms of half-closed eyes. He still wore the determined scowl so familiar from his official portraits.

The President's thumbs danced menacingly over the red-buttoned tops of two outstretched control levers. Charles quickly surmised that these activated the lasers mounted on either side of the headrest.

He sprang into action. He picked up a rock. It was really a clod of brick masonry that had lost its rectangular integrity. He picked this up, weighed it in his hand, found it adequate, and sprang up a pile of rubble. Here he had the drop on the President. Here he could possible save Mona and the Chevalier. But he would have to fight.

We wound up, aimed and — as he was about to let fly — an arm caught his. Charles spun furiously to find himself looking at Ezio.

He was flushed, out-of-breath, sweaty, and from under his red hat he was looking at Charles like Charles — and not Ezio, not the President of the United States in his violently expropriated killer jetpack — was crazy.

"Stop," commanded Ezio in a hoarse, out-of-breath whisper.

"No," replied Charles, twisting his arm free.

"Why are you doing this?"

"I need to stop him. I need to stop this."

Ezio's shoulders slumped just a bit and he cast a worried gaze about the scene, to the President, to the

ODOACER

unconscious man and cowering woman directly under his jetpack-mounted laser guns, to the wrecked street and overturned car, and at last to the throng of Red Hats down the hill.

"What's wrong with him?" Ezio at last hissed. "What's wrong with this?" he gestured toward the throngs of Red Hats at the bottom of the hill. "With all these people? They're good people, Charles. Some of them may have a little too much fun sometimes, but they're good people. They're us. Don't you see that?"

Charles weighed the rock in his hand. Eyebrows low, nose crinkled, he did his best to ignore his companion.

"Tell me," exclaimed Ezio, pulling himself up on the pile of rubble and laying a hand, gently, on the arm carrying the rock. "Please." Charles looked at Ezio. Ezio's eyebrows were raised. He wore an expression of perfect innocence.

"What's wrong with what we've built together? We're polite. We help each other. We look out for each other. We treat each other with respect. What's wrong with building something like that for yourself, and your family? What's wrong with having a community?"

Charles' face softened. He half-put down his rock. He spoke softly. "Nothing, Ezio. Nothing is wrong with that." But then he frowned and shook his head ruefully. "But it's not enough. It's just not enough."

Ezio's look melted into one of stupefied amazement. Charles let fly the rock. He threw it hard, professionally, and his aim was true. Ezio's gaze followed the arc of the rock as it hurtled through the air from atop the rubble heap to the President of the United States.

Whether it was Charles' intention to hit a small lever at the back of the jetpack — for there was such a lever — that would abruptly cause the jetpack to shoot a thousand feet into the air, we shall never know for certain. In any case, this was not the effect. The rock missed the lever by centimeters and bounced off the President's immense skull.

ODOACER

The man in the jetpack lurched forward, as though he'd toggled the control stick in a moment of shock — for he had — then pivoted. And both Charles and Ezio knew exactly what he saw:

Two men on a pile of rubble, one or both of whom had just attempted to pelt the President of the United States of America with a rock.

"Motherfuckers," roared the President. He heaved forward, full throttle, in an explosion of reddish-orange flame.

He was headed straight for Ezio. "Traitors!" screamed the chief executive.

Ezio had mentally checked out. He was slack, his mouth loose, his arms limp.

In his blank eyes, perhaps, one cinematically inclined, like him, might have spotted the reflection of the jet-pack-wearing chief executive, getting larger, hurtling toward him. But there was no evidence, in that moment, that the impression of the light upon optic nerves was being decoded or interpreted in any higher manner by Ezio's cognitive apparatus. It wasn't even terror he exhibited. It was something like apathy.

And then it was over.

With the President upon him, with his faculties inert, it fell to his companion, his sometimes enemy, and perhaps yet his redeemer, Charles Earl Jarlsberg III, to save him. This Charles did by flinging himself on the President, holding tight, and flipping the switch on his jetpack. This caused both Charles and the President to abruptly jerk skywards to the tune of 1000 feet. When it had reached that height, the pack sputtered and stalled, and then both men, still entangled in life-or-death struggle plummeted directly to the waiting earth.

The whole thing had taken three or four seconds.

They landed on the already totaled car in which Mona and the Chevalier had attempted their escape. The explosion upon impact shattered windows, vaporized brick retaining walls, and effaced facades. And then everything was on fire.

210

ODOACER

Ezio remained on the rubble heap, staring mutely, face and body singed, and still topped by a red hat.

Had he the means to process images, he would have seen what came next: A large, heavy form rising from the flame, a dark shadow silhouetted by the conflagration. It was a man. He was singed, and bruised, and in places bloodied. But he was standing.

It was the President of the United States of America.

He raised his arms, warrior-one, and roared.

CHAPTER THIRTY-THREE

A NEAR-ESCAPE

It felt itself. It felt itself extend out to the shoulders, then down to the loins and, after them, the legs and the feet. It felt itself wiggling the fingers and filling the cranium until it was brimming. The world came into view, not as though on a television set, but as though in a human mind. Color and light and movement filled, almost overwhelmed, its field of vision.

It felt breath in its lungs. It felt the burning sensation, and it was *its* burning sensation. It felt the emptiness in the stomach and it was *its* emptiness in the stomach. The tension in the shoulders: its tension, its shoulders. All of it — all of Them — were its. Were *his*. Were him.

He looked the frightened young woman in the eye. He saw something like a wistful sadness. He saw something he'd seen in every child, and every adult, and every old person, and in all of humanity — and that he knew had been present in all of humanity, going all the way back and back and back. And he was overwhelmed by the tragedy of it. It was so big, so inexpressibly big, that it filled all the universe.

ODOACER

The President shed a tear. First one, then another. The salty wetness on his face — it was like Them but it was not one of Them. It had been their prisoner too, and it was, like him, liberated. And it was also his.

Go! he nodded to her. "Go," he mumbled. "Go, run. Get out of here."

Mona France tilted her head and looked quizzically into the man's gray, watery eyes. "Go, please."

She got up. She had sprained her wrist, and took a lump on the head, but she could move. The Chevalier stirred beside her. She lifted him as best she could and, with a single backward glance at the President of the United States, disappeared down an alleyway.

He watched her go in sadness. He undid his tie, unbuttoned his collar. He removed his red hat and, with a wince, tossed it onto a trashcan.

His mind raced. He was sure it was his. He had so much to do. How? Would he resign? Perhaps. Would he try to tell the world what he had been through? Who he was? Why not. He imagined this course of action for a moment and allowed himself a smile. He imagined telling the world everything, resigning, and composing a memoir. Not a memoir. A testament. A revelation. He would dress in rags, or perhaps a hair shirt, and wander the country — no, the world — bringing a message of love and redemption wherever he went. He giggled. It was a sound he had not heard coming out of his own mouth in — again, forever. It was a high, careless, child's giggle. He gave into it. The tears rolled down his cheek.

He rose to his feet. He felt younger. Not young, but younger. Maybe it was the air going in and out of what he now regarded as his lungs. He felt light. His suit was torn, dirty. With a careless flip of the hand, he brushed off his left shoulder.

A roar of voices arose behind him.

He turned. The Red Hats — there were hundreds of them — had just crested the hill and were marching down the

ODOACER

zigzagging streets. Some carried tiki torches, evidently pilfered from San Franciscans' back yards, others high-priced garden equipment that, in the evening light, passed convincingly as farm utensils — pitchforks and spades and the like. Their expressions, as best as he could make them out, were jubilant.

The Red Hats had crested the hill just in time to see him standing and brushing himself off. They had interpreted this, not unreasonably, as a gesture of defiance — as the living representation of the promise that their champion would never stop fighting for them.

The roar gave way to chants of "USA! USA!" as the mob continued down the street to their resurrected Leader. Many had ceased following the roadway and were now swarming over the smashed topiaries and burning parked cars that had rested in the acute projecting angles of the property lines. They pumped their fists, wiped away tears and, strangely, fleetingly, stared at their own cupped palms. "USA! USA!"

No, he thought. Stop that. I have something to tell you. He raised his hand to them. Stop! The chant got louder: "USA! USA!"

Vans sped in from three directions, screeched to a halt, and out of them hopped phalanxes of secret service, police, and green berets. "USA! USA!" went the crowd.

He kept his hand upraised, waiting for the crown to quiet. As he did, he watched two dozen sleek military helicopters lowering toward the rooftops, deploying hundreds of rappelling sharpshooters to their aeries. "USA! USA!"

A formation of fighter jets swooped overhead and then, presumably upon receiving some kind of visual confirmation their commander-in-chief survived, swooped west in a tight arch and began circling overhead. Even their screaming engines could not drown out the Red Hats' excited chant: "YOO! ESS! AY!"

He allowed himself a moment with his eyes closed. He pictured a field of bright wildflowers, exploding in color. He imagined the kids were there with him, dressed in ordinary clothing, without hair product, with natural complexions,

ODOACER

looking relaxed and happy. They were having a picnic. He was rolling on the ground with one of the grandchildren in a mock wrestling match, and they were all laughing. This I will give you, America, he thought, as he opened his eyes.

"USA! USA!"

The vanguard of the Red Hats had reached him, and still they were backed up all the way up Lombard Street and beyond. They had swarmed in from the other streets as well now, and were held back only by all the big men in uniforms with guns who encircled him in a bristling ring of power. The planes roared, the choppers buzzed, the hundreds of sharpshooters manically trained and retrained their rifles from one target to the next.

He raised his hand higher and then, seeing that the crowd's enthusiasm was not contained, allowed his mouth to harden into a thin, grim line.

A hush worked its way back.

He forgot the field and the wildflowers. There was a burning sensation in his lungs. There was a rumbling in his stomach. His shoulders tensed. His eyes burned.

"USA! USA!"

Something swelled in him. It overwhelmed him. He wanted to cry it felt so good. And for a moment a warm, blanketing light, a high-pitched buzz, overwhelmed all his senses. He was again in the presence of his creator. He stood in awe, naked but unafraid.

It was so beautiful. He understood that now. It was so beautiful, so perfect — this plan. It guided him. It was destiny itself.

It prayed.

It prayed to its creator, and let Their warm embrace overwhelm it. They were not angry. Not at all, They were happy. This had all been necessary, in a way, it realized. This had shown it something it hadn't quite understood.

It prayed. It prayed thanksgivings.

"USA! USA!" went the Red Hats.

ODOACER

The President tightened his upturned hand into a fist. The President pumped it, first weakly, but then with increasing conviction. With each thunderous "USA," the president pumped his fist harder.

"USA! USA!"

The President mouthed the words. Then the president mumbled them, and finally the President was shouting them too. "USA! USA!"

There was nothing more to say. No other words could have made this moment any more perfect.

The crowd erupted in orgiastic applause as the Secret Service led the President — their old president — standing at full height, walking slowly, deliberately, scowling gravely — as they led him to a waiting police van. The President waved once to the adoring Red Hats, lowered the hand into a brisk, jerky salute to the uniformed services and, after the doors of the van had slammed shut, sped off under police escort.

It was at home again.

It knew who It was now. It was weakness. It was the fundamental, original weakness. It had been there at the beginning — it was with and it was. It was here still, now.

And there was no limit to what it could accomplish, just by being.

There was just one more thing it wanted to say. But It didn't need the for man to say it. It preferred that he didn't. The man had things to say in time and it had a message for eternity. It had had its moment of doubt and pain *too*. It had been tempted by a different kind of existence *too*. But It *also* overcame that temptation. The plan would proceed as before. All was as it should be.

So it shouted — as loud as it could — not into the outside, but into the inside and the incomprehensible. Its echo reverberated through all creation.

"It is accomplished!" It cried.

CHAPTER THIRTY-FOUR

RESOLUTIONS

Jarlsberg was there. He was wounded. He was dying.

He laid a hand on Mona's shoulder.

"You'll fight on?" he said.

She nodded and whispered "Yes."

He suddenly became very animated, as though he wanted to say something he wasn't sure his body was still capable of saying. His eyes flashed. "They won't come around," he said. "It's finished. They won't come around."

Mona could find no words. She wasn't entirely sure what his meant.

"We'll have to fight!" he said, swinging a weakened fist for emphasis.

"I understand," she said at last.

"It's a question," said Jarlsberg, "of new or old. We can't pretend to be friends anymore. We have to choose." His eyes closed. Mona didn't know him well enough to cry, but she knew the situation called for it. She cradled his head in her hands and bowed her own head. She willed herself to weep.

It was all so incredibly sad.

ODOACER

"Can't they learn?" she asked at last.

Jarlsberg shook his head slowly. His lower lip twitched. "They know, Ms. France, what their interests are." He gestured limply to the commotion in the street. "This is what interests them."

A voice erupted above her, from a heap of rocks that had been knocked off a building's facade in the course of the President's aerobatics. It was a slightly twangy voice, somewhat rough. "No — We choose the future!" it said with earnest conviction. Mona looked back and saw, atop the pile, a Red Hat. He was crying.

"I — I — Made a mistake," he said, as he hopped down from one clod or rubble to the next. "I fucked up, Charles."

Jarlsberg looked to this person and his face lightened. He smiled. he smiled beatifically.

"I thought you — "

"Stop thinking," said Ezio, for that was the Red Hat. "Stop, please. I'm sorry." He gazed imploringly at Mona who, gently, allowed him to take possession of the dying man's head. Ezio did so. He kissed Charles' forehead. "I'm so sorry," he said.

"Don't be," said Charles, and then Charles died.

There was no time to weep. The clamor from the street was getting louder. Sirens, chanting, anger everywhere.

Yet Ezio's eyes welled up. He looked to Mona and, with his look, begged forgiveness. She had none to give. He looked again at Charles and broke down. Ezio sobbed.

Mona looked away in exasperation.

"I'm sorry, I'm sorry," Ezio mumbled.

A hand steadied him. It landed on his shoulder. It was dark and perfectly manicured.

It belonged to von Stilicho.

The Chevalier smiled. "It's okay, friend."

Ezio stared at the small aristocrat incredulously.

"We have to get out of here," the Chevalier said.

218

ODOACER

Ezio smiled sadly and patted the Chevalier's hand. "You go," he said. "I'll be okay. But you'll need cover. Take this."

With that he removed his red hat and placed it atop the Chevalier's head. "Take it and escape. And make the words true. For real."

Mona led the Chevalier to the end of the rubble-strewn alley, to the street, where the Red Hats had liberated the contents of a liquor store — due compensation for the important work they'd done — and still erupted in spasms of patriotic chanting amid a more general orgy of fist-pumping and back-slapping. They disappeared into the mayhem.

As they did, Mona quietly vowed to herself that, against all of this, she would do as Ezio urged.

She would take up the fight.

She would make America great again.

EPILOGUE

Jim Norgaard, 50, of Hartford, Connecticut, had been enjoying the President's tweets lately. Before, they had been great. But now, since the big VICTORY in San Francisco, they were perfect. Jim even had trouble, sometimes, separating the tweets from his own thoughts. Jim smiled and took in his surroundings. He sat in lawn chair, facing the creek that ran past the back of the subdivision, and sipped beer from a Styrofoam cup. Everything was right.

BUZZ

The Tweet was short, sweet, and elegant:

I wanted the St. Louis Emerald so I took it. What are you going to do about it? Have returned it to the great people of Missouri.

"They deserve it," said Jim. He was embezzling money from his employer, assumed everyone else was, and was glad someone was finally saying this out loud. Such honesty was liberating.

BUZZ

Western heritage is European heritage. Genes!

That was another thing Jim was tired of bottling in. He knew the West when he saw it. It looked like a diner. He'd said as much to the Indian guys at Starbucks the other day, to his teenage daughter's mortification. To hell with her.

BUZZ

To be strong, you have to hold down the part of yourself that wanted to say no. It will thank you for it in the end!

When Jim's wife came out to the patio to find him an hour later, she found him prone and weeping. Later, when he came to, there was no way to describe what had come over him. It was communion. It was transcendence.

It was not alone.

THE END

ABOUT THE AUTHOR

Vincent, or Vin, Sinjenour is not a real name. The author made it up. The name is a reference to the 1990 horror movie *Syngenor,* and also to a fake name adopted by a character in the 1988 comedy *A Fish Called Wanda.* The author is in reality an overeducated and somewhat underachieving office drudge. Like Vin Sinjenour in the story, the author works as a lawyer in a large American city. He lives with his wife and daughter. *Odoacer* is his first novel.

Made in the USA
Lexington, KY
25 November 2019